"Why did you keep my name, Lindsay?"

She shrugged. "I assumed you knew I had."

"Your father didn't mention it," Gibb replied.

"I expect there are a number of things about me that my father felt were none of your business."

"Like your son. I suppose you're going to tell me he's my son, too?"

"I wouldn't dream of it. He just turned eight." Lindsay could almost see the calculation going on in his head. "Remember, Gibb? I divorced you because you were so opposed to the idea of having a child...."

Leigh Michaels has always loved happy endings. Even when she was a child, if a book's conclusion didn't please her, she'd make up her own. And, though she always wanted to write fiction, she very sensibly planned to earn her living as a newspaper reporter. That career didn't work out, however, and she found herself writing for Harlequin instead—in the kind of happy ending only a romance novelist could dream up!

Books by Leigh Michaels

Don't miss any of our special offers. Write to us at the following address for information on our newest releases.

Harlequin Reader Service
U.S.: 3010 Walden Ave., P.O. Box 1325, Buffalo, NY 14269
Canadian: P.O. Box 609, Fort Erie, Ont. L2A 5X3

The Daddy Trap
Leigh Michaels

Harlequin Books

TORONTO • NEW YORK • LONDON
AMSTERDAM • PARIS • SYDNEY • HAMBURG
STOCKHOLM • ATHENS • TOKYO • MILAN
MADRID • WARSAW • BUDAPEST • AUCKLAND

ISBN 0-373-03411-3

THE DADDY TRAP

First North American Publication 1996.

Copyright © 1996 by Leigh Michaels.

This edition published by arrangement with Harlequin Books S.A.

® and TM are trademarks of the publisher. Trademarks indicated with ® are registered in the United States Patent and Trademark Office, the Canadian Trade Marks Office and in other countries.

Printed in U.S.A.

CHAPTER ONE

IT WAS the first really nice afternoon of spring, and Lindsay Gardner had propped the door of her gift shop open to let the warm breeze flow through. The fresh air added a new tang to the spicy aroma of potpourri, which gave the shop its name, and it beckoned to Lindsay with almost irresistible force. Spring had always been her favorite time of year. She loved to walk barefoot through new green grass that was still tinglingly cold against her toes.

But she was alone in the gift shop today, and much as she'd like to hang a Closed sign in the door and go play hooky in the park, she had a shipment of china to unpack and inspect before she called the bride who'd ordered it. Then she needed to rearrange the display window, and on her desk was a stack of catalogs to look through to select the lines of merchandise she'd feature next Christmas. So she'd have to settle for the breeze and the sounds of traffic, which wafted in from the courthouse square through the open door, and let the park and the new green grass wait till Sunday, when Potpourri would be closed.

The bell that alerted the staff each time a customer entered didn't work with the door open, and Lindsay was so absorbed in checking each piece of china for defects that she didn't hear a thing till the woman who stood beside the cash register cleared her throat. "Excuse me—"

Lindsay jumped and turned around. "Oh, I'm sorry. Mrs. Harrison, isn't it? May I help you?"

The woman looked flattered that Lindsay remembered her name. "I hope so." She set a bulky shopping bag on the counter. "Someone told me that you take craft items to sell."

"Once in a while," Lindsay said cautiously. "When I have space." The qualification was correct, as far as it went, and it was far more tactful than the truth—which was that most of the crafts she was offered weren't the kind of quality she insisted on. "What sort of work do you do?"

"Oh, it's not me, it's my daughter. She works for your father over at the battery plant and just does this for fun." Mrs. Harrison pulled a bulky afghan from the shopping bag and spread it over the counter. "Up till now, that is. She thought maybe with the factory closing she'd better find something to help tide her over till another job comes along."

Lindsay blinked in surprise. So the rumor was flying that the Armentrout factory was closing. It was the first she'd heard of it, and it left an unpleasant emptiness in the pit of her stomach. There *were* difficulties at the plant just now, but her father had tried hard to be honest and upbeat with his employees, in order to keep any such fear from spreading. Apparently he'd been less successful than he'd thought.

"The factory isn't closing," Lindsay said. "There will probably have to be some reorganization, but—"

"That's what they say now," Mrs. Harrison interrupted firmly. "But whenever outsiders come in and decide what to do with a factory, you can just bet the news isn't going to be good. Not that I blame your daddy—I'm sure he's done the best he can with the economy the way it is, and I can understand why he'd rather let these efficiency experts he's brought in be the bad guys instead of doing it himself.''

Lindsay concluded she didn't have a hope of countering that argument. Mrs. Harrison had made up her mind. ''Well, I expect you'll be pleasantly surprised when the consultants' work is done,'' she said mildly and put out a hand to touch the afghan. It was a garish thing—broad stripes of lime green and royal purple ran the full length of the throw—but the yarn was soft enough even for a baby, and the workmanship was superb. ''What's this called? It's not crocheted, is it?''

''Nope, it's hairpin lace. Taffy said to tell you she can make all you can use.''

One in this color scheme would probably be a lifetime supply, Lindsay thought wryly. ''If she'd do commissions—I mean, let people choose colors to coordinate with their rooms and work to order...''

''I don't see why not. She doesn't care what color they are.''

That, Lindsay thought, was obvious. Perhaps the young woman was color-blind? ''Then ask her to stop and see me. We'll have to talk about price and some other details.''

Mrs. Harrison beamed. ''That's just great. You can keep this one in the meantime, and start taking orders.''

''That's very thoughtful of you.'' Lindsay waited till Mrs. Harrison was out of sight, then folded the afghan and put it on a shelf in the storeroom at the back of the shop. She couldn't put it on display till the agreement was firm—and in any case she'd have to think about how to show it to best advantage. It was certainly eye-catching. In fact, it would overwhelm any other merchandise in the vicinity.

But the afghan occupied only a corner of her mind. The rumor of the Armentrout plant closing was far more worrisome.

Lindsay had half a mind to call her father to warn him, but a glance at the clock stopped her. It was mid-afternoon, and it was also the first day on the job for the consultants Ben Armentrout had brought in to survey his business. For the next few days at least, until they were completely familiar with the entire plant, her father would have his hands full.

And—since Lindsay knew quite well that Ben had given his secretary orders that his daughter's calls were to reach him, no matter what he was involved in—she wasn't about to interfere. She'd catch Ben at home this evening. A few hours wouldn't make any difference, anyway; the rumor had probably been circulating for days already.

She finished packing the china shipment and called the bride, then took the window display apart. St. Patrick's Day was over, so the Belleek china with its shamrock pattern would go back on its regular shelf, and the leprechaun figurines and the green satin she'd used as a background would be put away in the storeroom till next year, to be replaced in the window by the pastels of springtime.

It had been a fairly quiet day up till that point—typical for the middle of the week—but as soon as Lindsay started trying to concentrate on the new window display, people began appearing in an unsteady stream, and she was continually having to climb out of the window to wait on customers.

"Not that I'm complaining," she told the big black cat who'd wandered down from the upstairs apartment during a momentary lull. "Every one of them bought something, which means I can afford your food next week. Aren't you pleased to hear that, Spats?"

The cat yawned and washed his already immaculate white paws.

Lindsay laughed, climbed into the window once more and began arranging two elegant porcelain dolls at a tiny table draped in pink and topped with a delicate china tea service. She was fluffing a dainty satin costume when the bride came in to claim her china.

Lindsay leaned out of the window. "Hi, Kathy. Is school out already?"

"I didn't see you in there," Kathy Russell said. "And what do you mean *already*? Today was about three years long."

"I suppose with the weather so nice, all the kids had spring fever."

"Not only the kids—I couldn't wait to get away from my twenty-two eight-year-olds. And I see you had an attack, too." Kathy pointed at the open door with a smile.

"If I wasn't a grown-up, I'd challenge you to a few rounds of hopscotch." Lindsay started to climb out of the window once more.

"Since when did being a grown-up discourage you? Finish your decorating, Lindsay—I have to look for a retirement gift for one of the aides, anyway."

"Take your time." Lindsay turned toward the tea party. One of the dolls needed her hair combed....

From the corner of her eye, Lindsay caught a glimpse of a man crossing the wide street in front of the shop at an angle that suggested he had parked a car near Potpourri and was heading for the courthouse in the center of the square. She could see only his back—broad shoulders, slim hips, long legs, dark hair—but the sight made her gasp, and her heart gave a painful jerk.

How odd it was, she thought, that after nearly nine years, she still reacted with such intensity to the fleeting sight of a man who vaguely resembled her ex-husband, or one who walked with the same kind of loose, ground-eating stride Gibbson Gardner had.

Kathy came toward the window, an ornate music box in her hand. "Are you all right, Lindsay? I thought you were choking."

"Oh—I'm fine." She was a bit breathless, though, and Kathy didn't look convinced. Lindsay tried to laugh it off. "It was nothing, really. I just saw a guy in the square who looked a bit like Gibb, and for a split second I thought I was going to have a heart attack."

As soon as the words were out, she regretted them. She never mentioned Gibb any more, and no one else ever brought up his name, either—at least not in Lindsay's presence. It was almost as if he'd never existed, and that was just fine with her. The last thing she wanted to do was leave the impression, even with her best friend, that she still had Gibbson Gardner on her mind.

"Anyway," Lindsay added easily, "my momentary hallucination is now past." She gestured at the delicate filigree box Kathy held. "That plays a Mozart piece. I'll wind it up if you like."

She climbed out of the window. It had been warmer than she realized in the confined space, with the sun bathing the plate glass; the cool breeze felt good on her flushed face.

Kathy handed over the box, listened patiently through the tinkling melody and nodded. "I'll take it. And my china, of course—I'm glad it arrived in time for my party Saturday night. You're coming, aren't you?"

"Of course." Lindsay started writing up the sale. "But I'd have thought that will be a paper-plate kind of crowd."

"Maybe you're right. I'll just stop at the supermarket for a steak and we'll initiate the china tonight."

Lindsay smiled. "Sounds like a great idea. If you've got a minute, I'll look for the original carton for the music box."

She dug through the neat stack of boxes under the stairs that led from the storeroom to her apartment above and found the carton. She was carefully packing the music box when Kathy asked, "Did you have a chance to ask your father about bringing my class out to tour the plant? Now that we've finished our unit on electricity, I think they'd enjoy seeing batteries being made."

Lindsay nodded. "He said it was fine with him, but the end of next week would be a better time. With the consultants starting to work—"

"Twenty-two third-graders underfoot is the last thing Ben needs. I can understand that. We'll make it Friday afternoon, then. Will you be able to help?"

"Sure—I'll be there. And I'll tell Daddy, so he can arrange a guide." She hesitated. "Kathy, have you heard any rumors about the plant closing?"

"No. Why?"

Lindsay told her about Mrs. Harrison. "I hate to upset Daddy about it if it's only a bee in the bonnet of one worker's mother. And she was wrong about other things, like calling the consultants efficiency experts. But..."

"If the rumor's floating around town, Ben needs to know," Kathy agreed. "I'll see what I can find out. I can ask without getting the attention you would."

Lindsay helped carry the boxes of china out to Kathy's car. She took her time walking back to the shop. She'd clipped her cordless phone to the belt of her tailored taupe slacks, and she was close enough to see if anyone walked through the door.

Besides, she thought, she hadn't even taken time out for lunch today, so she deserved a short break.

Winter's leftovers were still in evidence around the square. Sand coated the sidewalks, even though the ice underneath had melted. Across the street there were still a few stubborn humps of snow where the plows had pushed drifts out of the way after the last storm. But another day or two of pleasant warmth, followed by a nice spring rain, and Elmwood would be washed fresh and clean once more.

Across the street, in the center of the grassy square, the ornate county courthouse stretched three stories tall, topped with a wedding-cake tower that held Elmwood's largest clock. Facing the square, lined up with precision on all four sides, was perhaps the best collection of mid-Victorian commercial buildings to be found anywhere in the Midwest.

Lindsay thought the whole business district looked like a movie set, now that it had been expensively restored to its original appearance, with shops and offices downstairs and apartments above. She had never regretted her decision to locate Potpourri there, instead of in one of the new strip malls on the outskirts of town.

She paused in front of the window to study the display and decided the table needed to be turned slightly to present the tea service to best advantage. There was an empty spot in the corner, too, where she'd been standing—perhaps a nice display of picnic ware would fit in that awkward space.

The telephone clipped to her belt rang shrilly, and she answered it while she was still on the sidewalk. "Potpourri. This is Lindsay."

"Honey—"

"Oh, hi, Daddy. How's it going?"

"Do you have any customers?"

"Not at the moment." Lindsay frowned. She could hear tension in Ben Armentrout's voice, and she wondered if the rumor she'd heard had gotten back to her father, as well. Or perhaps he was already frustrated by the consulting team.

"I tried to call you earlier but the line was busy," Ben said. "I need to talk to you, honey. Have you heard anything about Gibb?"

That was odd. Lindsay frowned and glanced over her shoulder. There were at least a dozen people in the courthouse square, but none of them was the man she'd seen earlier. He'd be long gone by now, of course—and he probably wasn't at all like Gibb, really. Perhaps she'd been having sort of a psychic flash—it wouldn't be the first time she and her father had found themselves thinking about the same thing at the same time.

But why Gibb?

Daddy's heard some news, she thought. It had never happened before, but it wasn't unreasonable that someone who'd known both Ben and Gibb from the old days might have called Ben Armentrout to tell him that his former son-in-law had been promoted, or married, or seriously injured...

The sudden frozen fear Lindsay felt took her by surprise. She and Gibb had parted nine years ago with harsh words and harsher feelings, and there hadn't been a single contact since. It made no sense at all for her to feel panicky over the possibility of bad news about him—

though she supposed that the mere fact he had once been important in her life was enough to explain the breathless sensation. She'd feel the same if she got bad news about any of her friends.

"I haven't heard anything. What's going on, Daddy?"

Ben Armentrout sighed. "He's here, Lindsay."

She was stepping across the threshold as he spoke, and the shock turned her knees to rubber. She caught herself with a hand on the edge of the door. That was the only thing that kept her from falling.

Gibbson Gardner was in Elmwood.

Lindsay's head was spinning, and she seemed to be hot and cold all at the same time—her face felt flushed, but she was shivering. She swallowed hard and sank down on the window ledge, clutching the telephone in a death grip.

For the first year after their divorce, she'd worried about him coming back. She'd even had nightmares now and then about what she'd do if he reappeared. But long ago she'd concluded that Gibb would never be coming back, because whatever it was he'd felt for her had been destroyed in the fires of that last argument—in the same way that her love for him had been blasted into oblivion.

On the strength of that certainty, Lindsay had finally found peace. She'd rebuilt her life. She'd even forgiven him, though she knew she would never understand.

But to have him turn up now, after nine years—

"*Here?*" Her voice was drenched with fear. "Are you sure?"

"I've seen him, Lindsay."

"He came to the plant? What does he want? Why is he here?"

"We can go into the details later," Ben Armentrout said firmly. "The reason I'm calling is that he asked if you were still here in town. I don't know if he was just asking or if he intends to seek you out, but I had to be honest, so—"

She interrupted. "Daddy, surely you didn't tell him about—"

A sudden fierce prickle on the back of her neck stopped her cold, and she jumped up from the window ledge and wheeled around.

Gibbson Gardner was standing just inside the open door, one hand on the jamb and the other in the pocket of his khaki-colored trousers. A navy sports coat was slung over one shoulder, and the top button of his white shirt was unfastened. His pose was as casual and easy as a dancer at rest, and he was watching her through half-hooded hazel eyes.

Lindsay wet her lips. "It *was* you," she whispered, hardly aware that she had spoken.

His eyebrows lifted a fraction of an inch. "Did your father tell me about what?" His voice was low, but there was a hard edge to it that she well remembered. He'd sounded just the same way on the evening of their last, most bitter quarrel.

Lindsay remembered she was still holding the phone. "I have to go, Daddy," she said. Her voice was tight with strain. "I'll talk to you later." She pushed the button that broke the connection and laid the phone down in the window as carefully as if it was made of spun sugar.

"What is it you don't want me to know, Lindsay?" Gibb asked.

For one split second, Lindsay contemplated making a run for it. If she could dash through the store and up the stairs to her apartment—

But she couldn't, of course. She knew that despite the indolence of his pose, Gibb was as alert as a runner at the starting blocks. And what would she gain by running, anyway? It would be far better to stay and face him down. Nothing she did was his business any more. He'd given up that right nine years ago, when he'd turned his back on her.

She squared her shoulders and put up her chin. "Hello, Gibb. You haven't changed a bit, have you? You're still nasty and suspicious."

But he had changed. He was almost thirty-five now, and though he was every bit as lean and muscular as she remembered, there were fine lines around his eyes and threads of silver at his temples. The seriousness that had sat so uncomfortably on the young man she had known had settled into confidence—as if he had tested himself and was comfortable with the results, and no longer felt he had anything to prove.

"You haven't answered my question," he said.

"I don't owe you any answers. Remember? Or shall I go and dig out the divorce decree to remind you?" Lindsay went on the offensive. "Why are you here, anyway?"

"Your father told me where to find you."

"So you came running right over? Well, it's very thoughtful of you to stop in to say hello," she said with mock sincerity. "Though after nine years, I can't think why you'd believe I was interested in where you go or what you do."

She hadn't thought it was possible for his eyes to grow harder.

"There's no reason you should be interested." His voice was cold. "I'm not here to make a stab at a joyous reunion."

"You relieve my mind. What do you want, Gibb? Or have you already discussed your needs with Daddy, and you just stopped to say goodbye as you leave town again?''

''My needs being money, I suppose you mean?''

She'd half-expected that he'd take offense at the implication, but his tone was smooth. Lindsay shrugged. ''I didn't say that.''

''You sound very matter-of-fact about it, though. Is Ben still buying your way out of all your mistakes, Lindsay?''

She gritted her teeth and kept her voice level. ''I wouldn't throw stones, if I were you. He may have paid you to get out of my life—but you took the money.''

''And therefore I must be blackmailing him—or you—for more now. Is that what you think?''

''You haven't given me any other reason for bothering me.''

''I stopped because I thought it only polite to tell you that I was here, instead of letting you hear it through the grapevine.''

Elmwood's oh-so-efficient grapevine, Lindsay thought bitterly. Oh, the gossips would have a wonderful time with this—if he stayed in town long enough for the word to get around.

''Well, now that you've done what you set out to do...'' She made no effort to hide her glance at her wristwatch.

His hazel eyes didn't leave her face; she knew it, though she wasn't looking at him. His voice was lower, quieter, but not a whit softer. ''What are you trying to hide, Lindsay?''

''I don't have anything to hide.''

''Being defensive is no way to convince me of that.''

And it was no way to get rid of him, either, she thought belatedly. He was mulish enough to stay right there till he got some sort of answer.

That was another thing that had changed, she reflected. Not his stubbornness—determination, she was convinced, had been a congenital condition with Gibbson Gardner—but the way he exercised his will. He was much smoother now, much less dramatic...and even more inexorable.

"What didn't you want your father to tell me?"

She wished she knew exactly what Ben had said. But it was too late for that, so she looked Gibb straight in the eye and lied. "Where I was. I just didn't care to see you. But now that you're here, I suppose we might as well catch up on the news. How have you been?" she said with mock heartiness. "Have you been well? Are you happy? Tell me about the last nine years."

"Fine, yes, moderately, and I'll be happy to—if you really have enough time. But of course you do. The sign on the door says your shop will be open for another hour, and it's not as if customers are knocking each other down to get in."

Lindsay bit her tongue, hard. She hadn't stopped to think about the consequences of flippancy, and she was caught in her own trap. "Great," she said curtly, and moved toward the cash register. She could at least keep her hands busy, and then she wouldn't have to look at him. Maybe she could even keep from listening to him.

He followed her, looking around. "This is quite a nice shop."

"You sound surprised."

"Oh, no. Whatever you did, Lindsay, I'd expect it to be the very best." There was an infinitesimal edge to the words that robbed them of any compliment. "You always had a taste for the highest quality."

Except in husbands, she almost said. "And this way I can buy my own trinkets wholesale," she agreed, with a tinge of irony. "It saves me an incredible amount of money."

"And it gives you something to do with your time."

If he really thought she had no better reason for running a business than to fill her idle hours, Lindsay wasn't going to waste her time trying to convince him otherwise. "Oh, yes. The store makes a lovely hobby. It's so much more entertaining than needlepoint." She pulled a stack of bills out of the register and began counting them.

Gibb moved away to look at a display of crystal. "I'm surprised you don't have a few employees to do the actual work."

"As a matter of fact, I have several. Aren't you lucky to catch me here myself?"

Directly in front of Potpourri a car door slammed, and the bang resounded through the store. Lindsay looked up, and her heart sank.

The child who had gotten out of the car crossed the sidewalk in three steps and came through the door in a rush. His golden-blond hair was ruffled, and his jacket was only half-buttoned, crookedly. He skidded to a stop in front of the register and tugged a book bag off his shoulder. "Mom, can I go roller-blading with Josh and then have supper at his house? His mother says it's okay, and she'll bring me back in time to go to choir practice. She's waiting for me outside, so can I go? Please?"

Lindsay said quietly, "I have a customer, Beep."

The child drew himself up straight and looked around till he spotted Gibb. "Oh, I'm sorry. Excuse me, sir."

Lindsay nodded approval. "Thank you, dear."

Gibb came around the corner of the display shelves and stood with a crystal goblet in one hand, looking from one of them to the other.

If his eyes had been cold before, now they were frozen. "So that's what you didn't want me to know, Lindsay—that you have a son."

She wet her lips. "I have a son, yes, and it's not a subject I care to discuss with you. Beep is no concern of yours."

The little boy was looking back and forth between them, his forehead wrinkled.

"Did you call him Beep?" Gibb said. "What kind of a name is that?"

Beep looked a bit disgusted, but he answered politely. "It's a nickname. I'm really Benjamin Patrick, but I couldn't say it when I was little, and it came out Beep. Now everybody's in the habit." He looked Gibb up and down. "What's your name?"

Lindsay held her breath while Gibb seemed to think it over. The fact that he was hesitating didn't really mean anything, she tried to tell herself. He was probably debating whether to bother answering at all. Gibb disliked children, and he'd no doubt never encountered any quite like Beep. Of course, she had to admit, no one on earth was quite like Beep.

"I'm Gibb Gardner," he said, and Lindsay released her breath in a long and very quiet sigh.

Beep held out his hand for a formal shake. "It's nice to meet you, sir." Then he grinned. "That's pretty neat—we've all three got the same last name!"

Gibb's jaw set, and his eyes narrowed. So the news that his ex-wife was still using his name, and had passed it on to her son, had come as a shock, Lindsay concluded.

Beep wheeled to face Lindsay. "What about it, Mom? Can I go?"

She nodded. Somewhere, she'd seemed to lose the power of speech.

Beep dropped his book bag behind the register and dashed out to the waiting car, oblivious to the tension he left behind. He seemed to have taken all the air in the shop with him, for Lindsay was having trouble breathing, and when she looked at Gibb, his face seemed a bit gray.

It was a full minute before he broke the silence. "Why did you keep my name, Lindsay?"

She shrugged. "Isn't it obvious? I liked it better than Armentrout. Wouldn't anybody? And as long as I didn't have to put up with you..." She riffled a stack of twenty-dollar bills and tucked them into the bank bag. "I assumed you knew I had."

"Your father didn't mention it."

"I expect there are a number of things about me that my father felt were none of your business."

"Like your son."

"Beep certainly fits in that category."

"How old is he?"

She hesitated before she told the truth. "He's eight."

"That's interesting. I suppose you're going to tell me he's my son, too?"

"I wouldn't dream of it. He just turned eight." Lindsay could almost see the calculation going on in his head. "Remember, Gibb? I divorced you because you were so opposed to the idea of having a child that you wouldn't even discuss the subject. Why would I waste my time trying to convince you that Beep's yours? For the sake of child support, maybe?'' The sarcasm in her tone made it obvious that she thought the chances of collecting any would be nil.

The silence drew out for a long moment, and when he spoke Lindsay was surprised that there was neither anger nor relief in his voice, only matter-of-fact calm. "It didn't take you long to find another man after you got rid of me."

She nodded. "And it didn't take much of a man, either."

"That's obvious—since he didn't even stick around long enough to marry you."

"I didn't want him to. After my experience with you, I had no taste left for marriage."

"That makes two of us. We don't seem to be cut out for it, somehow—either you or me. And I suppose once you had what you wanted, a husband didn't matter much."

"I was happy to have my child, yes."

"A toy to play with. Your very own life-size doll."

"I certainly have no need to defend my decisions to you, Gibb."

He moved around the corner of the display shelves and put the crystal goblet carefully back into place. "Did I know him? Your son's father, I mean."

He sounded no more than idly curious, but Lindsay was not deceived. "Not very well, as I recall. And that's absolutely the last question I'm going to answer. Any say you had in how I live my life ended with our divorce, Gibb." She zipped the bank bag. "Now if you don't mind, I have work to do before I can go home. It's been very interesting, but I doubt we need to repeat this conversation—so don't feel you have to come back before you leave town."

He leaned against the counter. "Where did you get the idea I was just passing through?"

"I assumed, from what Daddy said..."

He raised one eyebrow and quoted her, dryly. "I expect there are a number of things about me that your father felt were none of your business."

She didn't want to ask. She didn't want to know. But the question escaped nevertheless. "Like what?"

Gibb looked her over slowly and then said with deliberation, "Like the fact that I'll be in town for a good while. A month or two, at least. Perhaps longer."

The bank bag slipped from Lindsay's suddenly nerveless fingers.

"You see, Lindsay," he went on quietly, "I'm the consultant who's going to be sorting out the problems at the Armentrout plant. So you'd better get used to seeing me around."

CHAPTER TWO

LINDSAY'S jaw dropped. "You're on the consulting team?" Her voice was hardly more than a croak.

Gibb shook his head. "Not exactly—I *am* the team. Triangle Consulting doesn't approve of a committee approach."

Lindsay was hardly listening. "I can hardly believe..." She stopped.

But Gibb picked up the thought. "Who would expect that a man who was once just a lowly assistant plant manager in Ben Armentrout's factory would be the one to come back ten years later to help him out of a bind? Is that what you were going to say?"

"Something like that," Lindsay admitted. "How did you get hooked up with Triangle, anyway? Daddy told me those people have a terrific reputation nationwide."

The corner of Gibb's mouth twisted a little. "Perhaps I lied about my qualifications for the job?"

"What? Oh. I didn't mean to insult you."

"Of course you didn't," Gibb said smoothly. "I'm surprised your father didn't tell you when you were talking to him earlier."

"You came in before he had a chance to. Though why he didn't tell me long ago, when he signed the contract—"

"He didn't realize I was associated with Triangle. I'm sure he'd have reconsidered if he had. As a matter of fact, I didn't know till last weekend that I'd be the one to take the assignment."

Lindsay said dully, "You don't sound too happy about it yourself."

"I've had better news now and then." Gibb's voice was dry. He picked up the bank bag she'd dropped and handed it back. "But a job is a job. I'll see you again soon, I'm sure. This is—unfortunately—a very small town."

After he'd gone, Lindsay stumbled to the storeroom and sat down hard on the nearest chair. After a while, though, the pounding in her ears eased, and the lump in her throat shrank enough that she could once more breathe without having to concentrate.

All in all, considering the kind of shock she'd had, things had gone reasonably well, she decided. Now that it was over, she was almost grateful that Gibb had sought her out. How much more difficult that encounter would have been in public! But as it was, the most difficult moments were behind them. No doubt they would meet again—as Gibb had said, Elmwood was too small to count on being able to avoid each other—but now there would be no need to do anything more than nod.

By the time Josh's mother dropped Beep off in front of Potpourri a little after six, Lindsay had regained her self-control and even a portion of her sense of humor. In fact, she was contemplating sending Gibb a formal note of thanks for stopping in to warn her.

Beep cupped his hands and peered in the glass door, and Lindsay went to unlock it. "Cutting things a bit close, aren't you?" she asked. "Choir practice starts in fifteen minutes."

"It was fun, though. I only fell down once, and Josh's mom took us out for hamburgers and fries."

"The fastest way to a young man's heart," Lindsay murmured. "How did soccer practice go after school?"

"Okay, I guess. Coach said it was too wet to use the field, so we had to practice indoors."

"It was nice of him not to send you home covered with mud."

"Oh, that wasn't why we didn't go out," Beep assured her soberly. "He said we'd tear up the grass if we did."

"I stand corrected. Bring your book bag, please, and put it in the storeroom so you don't forget to take it upstairs later."

Beep dragged the bag toward the back of the store as if it was far too heavy to pick up. "Mom, who was that guy?"

Lindsay didn't bother to ask which guy he meant. "Just somebody who's helping your grandfather out at the plant for a while."

"Why did he come to the store?"

"Because I knew him a long time ago, and he wanted to tell me he'd come back."

"Oh. I thought maybe he was my dad."

She ushered him through the storeroom toward the back door. "What would make you think that, Beep?"

The child shrugged. "I don't know. His name, I s'pose."

"Lots of people have the same last name," Lindsay said gently.

"I guess. But you hardly ever say anything about my dad."

This, Lindsay thought, was the last thing she needed. What a way to finish a trying day! But of course it wasn't Beep's fault. "I didn't realize there was anything you wanted to know."

"Sure. Lots of things. But you always look sad when I ask, and when I told Grandpa about it he said I shouldn't bug you. So I haven't."

Lindsay wanted to groan. She wanted her son to be able to approach her with any concern—but what if she couldn't answer his questions?

Before she could decide what to say, Beep dropped his book bag with a thump on the stairs that led up to their apartment and said, "Hey, that's pretty!"

Lindsay followed his pointing finger to the garishly striped afghan she'd left on the shelf. "Remind me to have your eyes checked," she said wryly, and the tense moment was past.

But she was still thinking about it three hours later when she went in to tuck him into bed. "Is the homework done?" she asked as she turned back the coverlet and fluffed his pillow.

Beep nodded. He was sitting at his desk in his pajamas, lower lip caught between his teeth, pasting together a paper kite he'd bought with his week's allowance. The project didn't look as if it was going well, Lindsay thought.

"Bedtime," she said gently. "The kite will wait till tomorrow."

He put the glue bottle down and climbed into bed.

Lindsay tucked the coverlet around him and turned off the lamps, then came back to sit on the edge of his bed. The streetlights from the parking lot behind the building provided just enough illumination to see the freckles that dusted his nose.

She stroked his hair, still damp from his bath and smelling of the strawberry shampoo he'd given her at Christmas, and said, "Beep, Grandpa was wrong when he said you shouldn't bother me with questions. If there's ever something you want to know—anything at all—you can ask me."

"Even if it makes you sad?"

"Yes. I may be sad sometimes—but I will never, ever be angry with you for asking about your father, or anything else."

Beep took that in and nodded slowly. "Mom..."

Lindsay braced herself.

"Could my dad make a kite?"

She wanted to laugh in relief, but she kept her voice steady. "I don't know, honey. I never saw him do it, but that doesn't mean he couldn't, I suppose."

"Oh. Good night, Mom. Love you." He was almost asleep by the time Lindsay was out of the room.

She made herself a cup of hot cider and sat down with the stack of catalogs she'd brought upstairs. The big living room was dim, lit only by the single floor lamp beside her favorite chair. There was little traffic on the courthouse square at this hour of the night, and the apartment was quiet. There was nothing to interfere with her concentration, except for her own thoughts.

She was a good mother; there was no argument about that. Beep lacked nothing—not even the so-called masculine pastimes. Lindsay had taught him to pitch a baseball and how to pick up a snake. She could keep on doing the things a father would as well as any man could.

But she had underestimated Beep himself. Because he hadn't asked about his father in a long time, she had assumed with relief that he didn't think about the subject any more. Now, abruptly, she realized that he was at an age to wonder. All his friends had fathers.

How easy it had looked, all those years ago when she had chosen to raise her child by herself. And how difficult, her intuition said, it might turn out to be before the job was done.

Gibb had barely looked around the apartment earlier that afternoon before he'd nodded his agreement to take it. It was far more elegant than his usual accommodations when he was on a job like this one. But furnished apartments were few and far between in Elmwood, the rental agent had told him, and so she'd talked her parents, who were taking an around-the-world vacation, into subleasing their home for a few months.

Gibb didn't particularly care. As long as the accommodations were clean and decent, he didn't give a darn about the details. As far as he was concerned, after years of hotels, any living space that provided a refrigerator and more than one room was luxurious indeed. He hadn't even noticed, till he started setting up his laptop computer on a table near the front windows, that he had a perfect view of the front of Potpourri, just around the corner on the courthouse square.

Not that it mattered. He had a whole lot more important things to do in the next two months or so than watch Lindsay.

He turned on the computer and pulled up the spread sheets that detailed the financial position of Armentrout Industries. Once it had been a primary manufacturer of batteries of all sorts. Now it was no wonder Ben was concerned—his business was beginning to hemorrhage cash. The problem was deciding if and how the process could be reversed.

Gibb leaned back in his chair and tapped his fountain pen gently against his front teeth.

The near-silence bothered him. His last few assignments had been in big cities where nothing was ever quiet, and Elmwood would take some getting used to. He walked over to the entertainment center, flipped through a stack of compact disks and selected several.

With the soft strains of a Mozart symphony filling the air, he was just settling into his chair when he heard a car door bang down in the square. He glanced out and saw a small shadow crossing the sidewalk to look in the door at Potpourri.

The lights in the shop were still on, but it was obviously closed, for he saw Lindsay unlock the door to let the child in. Was it his imagination, or was the square really so quiet that he could hear the warm murmur of her voice?

It was you, she'd said, when he came into the store. She'd sounded as if she'd spotted a ghost—but she must have seen him on the square earlier, when he'd been on his way to look at the apartment.

How little she had changed in nine years. She'd been pretty at nineteen, with her golden-blond hair and wide-set brown eyes. Now that the girlish roundness was gone from her face, letting the exquisite bone structure show to advantage, she was beautiful. But he had no doubt she could still be a fire-spitting hellcat when someone got in her way. Even if she hadn't quite lost control of her temper this afternoon as she used to do, it was obvious that she was as sensually passionate as ever. Maturity and responsibility had provided a veneer, but underneath the surface Lindsay Armentrout was the same unpredictably bubbling cauldron of hot lava that he'd fallen in love with so long ago—and that had burned him so badly.

But of course there was one very important difference in her life—the child she had craved as a little girl wants a doll. The child Gibb couldn't give her.

Her son had just turned eight, she'd said. Gibb's mental calendar told him that she had waited only three or four months after he'd left Elmwood before she'd taken up with her child's father.

Or maybe she hadn't waited at all.

Not that it mattered, of course. No one would ever describe Gibbson Gardner as a sentimental fool, and he'd long ago consigned not only his marriage but everything that went with it to a mental scrap heap. All that was long done with.

He'd told Lindsay the truth this afternoon—he'd stopped to see her purely out of good manners, to tell her himself that he was back, rather than let her hear via the town's gossip. Now that was past, and he had other things on his mind.

The lights inside Potpourri blinked off. They must be going home.

Did she still live in the apartment above Ben Armentrout's carriage house, where she and Gibb had spent the troubled months of their brief marriage? Or, by now, had Ben built her a new house in the best neighborhood in town? Lindsay had always loved the best, and Ben had always leaped to provide it. That had been the source of their last and most horrendous quarrel.

"And maybe that's what's wrong with Armentrout's financial status now," Gibb said aloud. With new determination he turned his attention to the spread sheets. He'd seen a listing in there for something called the Armentrout Trust; was that where Lindsay was getting the money to maintain her lifestyle and run her exquisite little shop?

*   *   *

Ben Armentrout called Lindsay before Potpourri officially opened the next morning. "Are you still speaking to me?" he asked bluntly when she answered.

"Oh, Daddy—yes, of course. It's not your fault."

"Well, after the way you hung up on me yesterday, I wondered. And I did sort of invite him, so—"

"But you didn't know what you were doing." Lindsay finished arranging change in the cash register drawer and closed it. "And I only hung up on you because Gibb came in. Are we having lunch today, or will you be tied up?"

"Of course we're having lunch," Ben said heartily. "It's Friday, isn't it? I wouldn't miss taking my gorgeous daughter out to lunch at the Willows on Friday— no matter what else is going on."

"You won't mind if I meet you at the restaurant today instead of picking you up at the plant?" Lindsay's voice was casual. "My helper isn't coming to work till noon."

"I completely understand," Ben said blandly.

He was waiting for her at his favorite corner table at the Willows when Lindsay came in, with a martini already in his hand and the menu open. A big bear of a man with a barrel chest and a shock of iron-gray hair, he stood up to give her a hug and looked at her shrewdly over his half-glasses as he sat down once more. "Well, you seem to have survived the shock."

Lindsay didn't pretend to misunderstand. "I didn't have much choice. He was just there all of a sudden. But it wasn't so bad, really—we got the worst out of the way. I don't think we'll be seeing much of each other."

"Especially if you avoid the factory," Ben murmured.

"The only real reason I have to go there is the Armentrout Trust, and if I could arrange for someone to drop off the mail to me, I wouldn't—"

The back of her neck startled to prickle, and automatically she reached to rub it. Then she remembered the last time she'd felt that itchy sensation, and with a feeling of foreboding she glanced toward the door.

Gibb was standing there, surveying the dining room as if he was looking for someone.

Lindsay sank back in her chair and tried to become invisible. "Daddy, did you invite Gibb to join this party?"

Ben almost dropped his menu. "Of course not."

A slight hush fell over the dining room. Lindsay saw a few heads turning toward the door.

"Well, there isn't anything else to do but invite him now," she said glumly. "If we don't, the whole town will know it by dinnertime." She caught Gibb's eye and beckoned him over.

An elderly matron who was trailing the hostess to a nearby table saw the gesture and seemed to think it was intended for her. She paused beside Lindsay's chair and cooed, "Well, hello, there! I always think it's so sweet when a father and daughter go out for lunch together. Where's your little boy today, Lindsay?"

"He's in school, Mrs. Hanson."

"Oh, of course." The woman trilled a laugh. "How silly of me to have forgotten about school!"

It was no wonder, Lindsay wanted to say. It must be about a thousand years since Mrs. Hanson had been in school herself.

"Do you know, every time I see him he looks more like you," the woman went on. "Except that his hair is a little sandier, of course."

Gibb was standing beside Lindsay's chair.

Ben boomed, "Sit down, son."

"Son?" Mrs. Hanson asked, and turned to stare at Gibb. "Oh—I remember. You were Lindsay's husband once. Well, as I was saying, Lindsay, your little boy is very lucky to resemble you instead of his father. It's so fortunate, isn't it, that young Benjamin doesn't have—say—flaming red hair?"

Lindsay gritted her teeth and considered wadding up her napkin and gagging the woman with it. "Red hair can be so difficult for a man," she agreed sweetly. "My grandfather was a redhead, you know—almost a carrot top, in fact—so you're quite right to think I'm relieved that Beep isn't. But don't let us keep you from your lunch, Mrs. Hanson." She turned a cold shoulder toward the woman and smiled at Gibb. "Won't you join us?"

His eyebrows rose slightly. "I'm sorry to disappoint you, Lindsay, but I'm meeting someone."

"Oh." Lindsay felt deflated. *Who?* she wanted to ask, but she could imagine the incredulity in his eyes if she had the temerity to actually inquire. She added, with a touch of acid, "Don't worry about disappointing me, Gibb—I want to have lunch with you about as much as I look forward to a bleeding ulcer. I only meant there was no point in us looking like armed enemies. There's going to be enough talk as it is."

"Without a doubt," Gibb said. "So perhaps we should do our best to confuse the gossips."

Before she could anticipate his intentions, he'd bent over her, and his mouth was warm against the hollow of her cheek. It was really no more than a brush of his lips, but to Lindsay it felt as if eons passed while she sat there with a branding iron pressed against her face.

The hostess came back from seating Mrs. Hanson, and Gibb straightened up without hurry, asked for a table and followed her toward the far corner of the room.

"Well!" Lindsay said, and settled back in her chair. "If that isn't—"

She saw the two ladies at the next table lean toward her, obviously listening, and stopped dead, burying her face in her menu to wait for the murmurs to die down.

Ben was studying her with a puzzled look in his eyes. "What were you up to a minute ago, Lindsay? Neither one of your grandfathers had red hair."

"I know that. But Mrs. Hanson doesn't—so the next time she starts speculating about Beep's parentage, maybe she'll stop and think about it before she goes public." Lindsay didn't look up. "And by the way, what's this business about calling Gibb *son*? I didn't ask you to start the rumor that we're reconciling."

"You were doing a fair job of it yourself," Ben said mildly. "But considering who just joined him, I don't think you need to worry about it any more."

Lindsay couldn't help it; her self-discipline went straight down the drain, and she whipped around to look toward Gibb's table.

He was holding a chair for a tall, pencil-thin brunette in a purple suit and the highest heels Lindsay had ever seen. The woman was looking at him with a soft, intimate smile.

"Skye Oliver?" Lindsay whispered. "Where did Gibb meet Skye Oliver? She's only been in town a couple of years."

Ben shrugged. "He said something yesterday about going to look at an apartment."

"And she's a rental agent, so that figures. But why would he want an apartment?"

"He said he's tired of living in hotels."

"How long's he been living in them?"

"Why don't you ask him, Lindsay?"

"Because I really don't care—it was just an idle thought."

"Then don't expect me to interrogate him."

"Sorry." Lindsay held her menu a little higher and glanced over it at the couple in the corner. Gibb had seated Skye at his right, and she was leaning toward him with that same intimate smile, her hand on his sleeve.

She turned toward her father and said with an effort, "Daddy, Kathy Russell wants to bring Beep's class out to tour the plant next Friday afternoon."

Ben nodded. "That's fine. I might be able to take them around myself."

Lindsay heard Skye's tinkling laugh rise above the lunchtime murmurs and tried to ignore it.

My life has gone on, she reminded herself. It was only fair to assume that Gibb's had, too. He'd said he had no interest in marriage, not that he'd sworn off women altogether. And Lindsay didn't care, of course—it was just that she'd never given the matter any thought, so it was a bit of a shock to see it happening right before her eyes. Or perhaps she was simply suffering the aftereffects of that kiss he'd given her a few minutes ago.

What on earth was wrong with the man, anyway, to have pulled a trick like that?

"I'm never gonna get this put together right," Beep said, pushing his kite away in disgust. He planted his elbows on the worktable behind the cash register.

Lindsay closed the empty cash drawer and put the bank bag in the safe. "I'll help you with it after dinner," she promised. "Right now we need to go to the supermarket and run some errands, so get your sweater on."

Beep poked his lower lip out. "Do I have to go?"

"I know perfectly well you're capable of being on your own for a while. But *I'm* not ready to leave you alone for that long—so yes, you have to go. You can choose what you'd like for dinner, though."

"Candy bars and popcorn?" he offered.

"As long as it's chicken, fish or beef," Lindsay went on, as if she hadn't heard him. She pointed him toward the front of the store. "Wait by the door while I turn off the lights. We'll have to go out the front, because I left the car on the square this afternoon."

The bell on the front door tinkled just as she flipped the last switch. "Beep, don't go running off!" she called, and hurried across the dim display room to catch up with him.

"I'm right here, Mom." Beep sounded pained. "It wasn't me."

Gibb was standing just inside the front door, looking around. "I'm glad I got here before the store closed."

"You didn't," she pointed out. "I'm sorry, but—"

"I'm not looking for a gift."

"In that case, I'm really not sticking around to chat with you. I'll be here most of the day tomorrow, and I'll be at home in a couple of hours. The number's in the phone book if you want to call. But if you're here to apologize for the way you behaved at lunch today—"

"Not at all. That was a purely social kiss, and I've nothing to apologize for."

Lindsay didn't bother to argue the point. She just held the door open, with her key already in the lock. Beep marched out onto the sidewalk, and Gibb shrugged and followed.

"I want to talk to you about the Armentrout Trust," he said.

Lindsay turned the key and checked to be sure the lock had clicked. "What about it?"

"Tell me the details."

"Why not ask my father?"

"Because your name's on the paperwork as the administrator of the trust."

"That's right. He set it up that way because he thought it would be better if he wasn't the one actually doling out the money, but the trust is still his baby."

"Then you're just a figurehead?"

Something about the tone of the question made Lindsay uneasy. "Not exactly," she said slowly. "I make most of the decisions about where the money goes."

"All by yourself?"

"No. There's a board that approves what I do."

"Do they ever disapprove?"

"Of course they do. The minutes of the meetings are somewhere in Daddy's office—why don't you read them? They're public record."

"I will. Where does the money come from?"

Lindsay wanted to groan. Distracting Gibb from a topic he was interested in had always been slightly more difficult than changing the orbit of the moon. "A percentage of the profits of Armentrout Industries goes into the trust, and it's used for worthwhile purposes around Elmwood."

"Worthwhile by whose definition? Yours?"

"And the board's."

"Do these worthwhile purposes include things like maintaining a gift shop?"

"What?" Lindsay was incensed. "If you're implying I would divert charitable contributions for my own benefit—"

Beep gave a long and frustrated sigh and sat down on the front bumper of the nearest car. Lindsay was too furious with Gibb to notice that the car in question was a brand-new Lincoln, its showroom polish still gleaming.

Gibb said coolly, "Please don't do that, Benjamin."

"I'm not hurting it," Beep muttered. But he moved away from the car and started kicking at the base of a street lamp instead.

Lindsay glanced at the out-of-state plates and then at Gibb. "Your car?"

"Not exactly. It belongs to Triangle."

"And if it got scratched or dented, your boss would have your head? Perhaps I'd better take my son away so he won't breathe on it by mistake."

"Dammit, Lindsay—"

She took Beep's hand and started off down the street. She was walking fast, and he had to hurry to keep up. "Mom," he said plaintively.

Lindsay slowed her pace. "Sorry, Beep."

"You didn't *really* kiss him, did you?"

Lindsay sighed. She'd hoped he hadn't been listening to that part of the conversation. It was an unrealistic hope, she admitted. Like that of most eight-year-olds, Beep's hearing was highly selective. If he wasn't supposed to know something, he could catch a whisper from three blocks away, but if the subject was cleaning his room or taking a bath, a shout directly into his ear wasn't loud enough.

"No," she said. "He kissed me—sort of the same way that Great-aunt Ella kisses you at Christmas time."

Beep made a face. "Yuck."

Lindsay stifled a smile.

They were halfway to the supermarket when he spoke again. "I wouldn't want him to be my dad."

Lindsay watched him from the corner of her eye. "Any particular reason?" she asked carefully.

"Because you argue all the time, like Tommy's folks. It makes my stomach hurt to listen to them." He added flatly, "And besides, he doesn't like me. He yelled at me."

"Not exactly. He was a little blunt about it, but I don't blame him. I'm not wild about it when someone sits on my car, either. And you could have scratched it, you know. It's not that he doesn't like you."

Beep didn't look convinced.

She reached over to ruffle his hair. "Beep, honey— nobody could dislike you. He just doesn't know you, that's all. Now, what's it going to be for dinner?"

CHAPTER THREE

THE restaurant on the courthouse square looked no better or worse than many Gibb had patronized in his travels, but it was busy at midday on Saturday, which was a good sign. He took a seat at the counter, ordered almost at random and paged through the local newspaper while he ate his chicken-fried steak smothered in rich gravy with mashed potatoes and corn.

He was almost finished when Lindsay came in and perched on the edge of the seat next to him. She glanced at Gibb's plate and said, "You'll give yourself a heart attack, eating like that."

He gestured toward the sign in the window. "It says this is all home cooking."

"Well, maybe—if it's a home for the cardiac impaired." The waitress came over, and Lindsay said, "Three turkey sandwiches, on whole wheat, with tomato and hot mustard, to go." She turned to Gibb. "Don't let your food get cold for my sake."

He picked up his fork. "Would you like a cup of coffee while you watch me clog my arteries, or do you consider it poisonous, too?"

"I drink it now and then. But I told my assistant I'd be back in ten minutes." She was fidgeting with her necklace, a concoction of colored wooden beads strung on a leather thong. It was nothing like the expensive jewelry he would have expected her to wear—the kind she used to like so well—but then, perhaps she didn't flash the real thing when she was at the shop.

He signaled the waitress and told her to bring Lindsay a cup.

She stirred her coffee slowly and said, "Have you gone over the minutes of the Armentrout Trust yet?"

"A good many of them."

"Then I'll accept your apology for accusing me of mismanagement."

"That's very generous of you, Lindsay," Gibb said blandly, "considering that I haven't apologized."

Golden sparks of anger flared in her eyes. "You can't mean you still think I've been diverting the trust's money into my own pockets!"

"No. But I can't say I think the fund's been well-handled, either."

"Well, the next time there's a vacancy on the board, you can ask Daddy to nominate you to fill it. Until then, it's really none of your affair what the Armentrout Trust does with its money, is it?"

"True," he conceded. "As far as it goes." He speared the last piece of steak and savored it. "This is really rather tasty."

Lindsay shuddered. "If you consider that to be good home cooking—"

"You must admit I don't have much to compare it to."

"Well, if you live in hotels all the time... or are you talking about *my* cooking?" She bristled for a moment, and then a reluctant smile tugged at her lips. "It was pretty bad, wasn't it? Remember the night I tried to roast a chicken in the microwave and charred the bones?"

Gibb watched her mouth, bemused by the gentleness he saw there. "The one I will never forget," he said gravely, "is the apple pie."

He couldn't remember the last time he'd heard her laugh. He rather thought it had been long before that last quarrel.

"It would have tasted better with some sugar in it," she admitted.

The waitress appeared, folding the top of a brown paper bag, and Lindsay paid for her sandwiches. "Thanks for the coffee," she said, and was gone.

It was just as well, he reflected. Remembering the good times only emphasized the bad ones. He ought to know better than to encourage the memories.

He finished his coffee and sauntered across the square toward his apartment with his hands in his trouser pockets, enjoying the warmth of the sun on his face. The breeze carried a sharp edge, though, a curt reminder that it was still March and therefore unpredictable.

In fact, the weather was something like Lindsay— warm and charming one moment, furious the next.

In many regards, she'd still been a child when he married her—enchanting and delightful, but bent on having her way. Her mother had died long before, and she'd been Ben Armentrout's darling. At first Gibb, too, had indulged her. Then, as the weeks and months went by and her willfulness and his resentment increased instead of abating, he'd tried persuasion and logic, and finally—in the heat of that last quarrel—commands.

The strategy had backfired, of course. He should have expected that.

Lindsay had come home practically dancing with joy because she'd found exactly the furniture she had to have for their carriage-house apartment, and she'd bought it without waiting to ask Gibb because, as she pointed out to him, Ben Armentrout would pay for anything his daughter wanted.

Gibb had tried to explain to her a hundred times before that they needed to live on his salary rather than depend on Ben. This time he didn't bother to explain. He didn't even wait long enough for her to tell him precisely what she'd bought. He simply ordered Lindsay to cancel the purchase.

The quarrel didn't end there, of course—so it wasn't really accurate to say that their marriage had hit the rocks because of a bunch of furniture. If it hadn't been sofas or coffee tables or china cabinets or whatever it had been she thought she couldn't live without, it would have been something else; theirs was a marriage doomed to an early and unhappy end.

He'd accepted that fact long ago, and he'd hardly thought about it any more—until chance had brought him back to Elmwood.

Gibb was so far sunk in his thoughts that he didn't see danger approaching until something very like a cannonball hit him right above the belt buckle. He gasped, staggered, grabbed for his attacker—and looked down into the wide-set, deep brown, horror-filled eyes of Lindsay's son.

The child appeared to be dazed—or maybe he was just scared out of his wits. His shoulders, under Gibb's hands, felt bony and almost fragile.

It didn't take long for Gibb to deduce what had happened, for the evidence was almost directly underfoot. A cheap paper kite with a bedraggled tail lay on the sidewalk nearby, and Beep dropped a reel of string and rubbed the top of his head.

"Sorry, sir," he gasped. "I was just trying to get my kite up in the air, and I guess I was looking over my shoulder instead of watching where I was going."

Gibb's breath was still rocky. "Are you okay?"

Beep nodded. "I think so. Are you—are you going to tell my mom?"

Gibb squatted down beside him, his hands still on Beep's shoulders. "And get us both into trouble?"

The child looked puzzled. "You? Why would you be in trouble?"

"Well, I wasn't watching, either—and I must have walked straight into your path."

"Oh. It's different, though. She can't send you to your room," Beep observed solemnly.

Gibb was hardly listening. He was studying the small triangular face, so like Lindsay's. Beep had her big brown eyes, and the same soft, translucent skin. Lindsay didn't have freckles, though; he wondered if she had as a child, or if that was a legacy from Benjamin's father. The old biddy at the restaurant yesterday seemed to think the man had been a redhead, and the freckles would certainly follow. There *was* just a hint of red in the child's hair as the sunshine gleamed against it. Had he known any redheads, all those years ago? Several, he thought.

Beep's eyes had gotten even larger, and Gibb felt a small shiver run through the wiry little body. It was no wonder the child was uneasy, he thought, at being held and inspected by a stranger. Despite what Gibb had said about the accident being partly his fault, the kid might even think he was going to get a spanking right there in the courthouse square.

He let go of Beep's shoulders and straightened up, feeling a little uncomfortable. He hadn't a clue how to deal with children, and of course it showed. He didn't even know how to extract himself from the situation. He looked around, almost at random, and bent to pick up the kite. One of the balsa wood supports had cracked on impact with the concrete, and the paper cover was torn.

"I'm afraid your kite's ruined," he said finally.

He was half-expecting tears, but Beep only shrugged philosophically. "It's okay, I guess. It wasn't a very good kite, anyway. Even Mom couldn't get it put together just right. But it was all I could buy with my allowance."

The image of Lindsay bent over a cheap paper kite was enough to boggle Gibb's mind—the picture was nothing like the woman he remembered. "Your mother helped build it?"

He must have sounded incredulous, for Beep put his chin up a little. "My mom can do most anything," he said firmly.

"I'm sure you believe she can."

Beep squared his shoulders and looked up with a challenge in his eyes. "Why don't you like me?"

Gibb was taken aback. "I don't *dislike* you," he said cautiously. "I hardly even know you."

"That's what my mom said. But it feels like you don't like me."

From across the street, in the doorway of Potpourri, Lindsay called, "Beep! It's time for lunch!" and the child took off toward the shop without a backward glance.

Gibb couldn't tell if she'd even noticed him standing there; she didn't wave, and she vanished into the store's interior as soon as Beep had crossed the street.

He realized he was still holding the discarded kite, and called, "Benjamin, you left your—"

But Beep was already gone.

Why don't you like me? the child had asked.

Gibb could have given a dozen answers—all inadequate, each one of them leading only to more questions. The time for that kind of introspection was past. He'd long ago looked deep into his soul and accepted what was there, and it was too late to change the patterns of his life now.

He folded the broken kite and dropped it into the nearest garbage bin. As soon as it was out of sight, however, he felt guilty about disposing of it, in case Beep changed his mind and wanted it back.

Even if it hadn't been for the accident, the kite probably wouldn't have flown—Gibb had known that from a glance. But it had belonged to the kid. He'd bought it with his own money, he'd said. And for the grandson of Ben Armentrout, who could no doubt have anything he wanted just for the asking, that was saying something important.

There was a discount store across the block. Gibb had to look for a while to find exactly what he wanted, and by the time he walked into Potpourri with a bag, nearly an hour had passed.

A young woman he'd never seen before came toward him with a smile. "Good afternoon, sir. May I help you find something?"

"I'm looking for Benjamin," Gibb said, and then he saw the child, sitting at a table behind the cash register with a half-eaten turkey sandwich, a glass of milk and a comic book in front of him.

Beep turned around inquisitively as Gibb approached. He looked just a little wary.

"Don't fret, I haven't changed my mind about telling your mother," Gibb said under his breath, and opened the bag to draw out a colorful package. "This one's bigger and stronger." He handed it to the child. "And

I got everything you'll need to put it together, too. I think you'll find the right glue makes all the difference."

Beep looked at the package in his hands, and then at Gibb, and grinned. His eyes sparkled, and his front teeth—still too large for his childish face—gleamed. Inside Gibb's chest something twisted a little.

"The instructions are pretty good, too," he added hastily. "If you just take it step by step and—"

A shadow seemed to fall over Beep's face. "Won't you help me?"

Gibb glanced around the store. "Surely your mother—"

"She's busy up in her office. And it's a perfect day for kites." Beep looked through his lashes and wheedled, "If both of us work on it, maybe we could fly it yet this afternoon."

If he closed his eyes, Gibb could almost see the stacks of work waiting for him at the apartment. It was important work, and it was, after all, the reason he was in Elmwood at all. Buying the kid a replacement kite was one thing, but building and flying it didn't fit into his agenda anywhere.

"Please?" Beep whispered.

Gibb looked once more into the depths of those big brown eyes, reached for the package and tore it open. "Start reading the instructions," he ordered, and Beep settled happily in his chair and began.

The afternoon sun was slanting in the west window of Lindsay's office when she finished with the last catalog and stood up to stretch. Christmas would be an exciting season, with the new merchandise lines she'd chosen. It might be the biggest sales month she'd ever had.

But there would be plenty of time to dream of increased sales after the merchandise arrived. Just now she had other things to do—Kathy Russell's party was tonight, and unless Lindsay got busy, she'd be late.

She put a chicken breast under the broiler for Beep's dinner and phoned downstairs to ask her assistant to send him up to the apartment.

"He's out on the square with his kite," the young woman said. "I'll call for him if you like."

"Never mind, I'll just lean out the window." Lindsay opened one of the casements at the front of the apartment and looked out. On the sidewalk across the street, Beep was lying flat on his back, legs crossed at the ankles, watching a bright red kite, which soared far above his head. When she called his name, he got to his feet immediately and started slowly reeling in the string, but it was a quarter of an hour before he came up the stairs.

"Taking your time, aren't you, buddy?" she said. "Hurry and wash your hands, or your dinner will be cold."

"You can't just pull a kite down in a minute," Beep argued. He slapped water on his face and grabbed a towel. His voice was muffled. "Gibb said if you try to reel it in too fast, you'll crash it for sure."

Lindsay's heart seemed to thud to a halt. *I can't be hearing right*, she thought. Gibb, giving advice on kite flying?

She looked at the kite Beep had laid carefully on the end of the kitchen table. "I thought your kite was blue," she said.

"It was. But I wrecked it."

"Where'd this come from, then?" Her voice was carefully casual, and she didn't look directly at him but at the plate she was dishing up. "I thought you spent all your allowance on the blue one." Did she have a preadolescent shoplifter on her hands? Kids Beep's age had been known to simply take what they wanted.

Beep nodded. "I did. Gibb bought this one for me."

"What?" Lindsay almost dropped a spoonful of green beans.

"I didn't ask him to, Mom." Beep sounded impatient. "He bought it because he sorta helped wreck the other one. It flies really great, too."

"I noticed." She told herself not to overreact. If Gibb had damaged the kite, she couldn't be petty enough to refuse to allow him to replace it. Though how, she wondered, did one *sorta help wreck* a kite? Or did she even want to know?

Maybe, she thought wryly, *I'd rather deal with the shoplifting problem*.

"I think he likes me after all, at least a little bit," Beep said contentedly as he cut the first bite of his chicken. "Once he got to know me, it was just like you said, Mom."

With her head swimming with confusion, Lindsay left Beep eating his dinner and went to take a shower. She hadn't dreamed of this sort of complication. She certainly hadn't foreseen, when she'd tried to reassure Beep last night, that instead of leaving the man strictly alone he might actually set out on a campaign to convince Gibb he was likable—but that was what it sounded as if he'd done.

And where was that likely to lead? To nothing good, Lindsay was certain of that. If he didn't succeed, Beep was going to be hurt. And if he did succeed—

Don't jump to conclusions, she warned herself. Gibb had given the child a five-dollar kite and taught him to fly it. It was no big deal. Still, she'd have to make sure Beep understood that Gibb would not be in Elmwood for long, and that his business would keep him far too busy to make friends with an eight-year-old kid.

She pulled her new rust-colored sweater out of a drawer and paired it with matching tailored pants. The teenage baby-sitter had arrived by the time Lindsay was dressed, so she simply kissed Beep on top of the head, reminded him not to play with his dinner and reached for her lightweight spring coat. "The number's on the notepad beside the phone in case you need me," she told the sitter. "I don't think I'll be late."

Beep poked at a bite of chicken. "You smell pretty, Mom."

"Thank you, dear. It must be the shampoo you gave me."

"And you look nice, too," the sitter said. "Are you meeting your date at the party?"

"It's not that sort of party, just a sort of drop-in get-together to initiate Kathy's new house."

The sitter shook her head. "I don't know what's wrong with the men in this town, letting you go to a party by yourself."

Lindsay didn't bother to explain. A teenager for whom a dateless party was a disaster wasn't likely to understand that Lindsay often preferred to go alone. Life was a whole lot less complicated that way.

Beep was twirling his fork, frowning at a green bean impaled on it, when she left. Lindsay wondered what he was thinking about and made a mental note to take him for a long walk tomorrow and see if she could find out. If it was Gibb he had on his mind, the sooner she disillusioned him, the better.

The party had already started when Lindsay reached the big old square house Kathy and Ian Russell had bought. Kathy met her at the front door and exclaimed over the basket Lindsay handed her.

"Salsa and chips and gourmet cheese—I'm going to put these back for Ian and me," she decided. "This bunch of barbarians would snap them up in two minutes."

Lindsay glanced around at the crowd. "How many people are here, anyway?"

"I've lost count—but we invited about a hundred of our nearest and dearest friends. You haven't seen the house since we moved, have you?"

Lindsay shook her head. "It was totally bare last time I was here."

"Well, it's not much better now. We don't have enough furniture, and we can't afford to buy any just now." She pointed into the huge living room, which was occupied only by a stereo set, a couple of enormous green plants and a small crowd of party-goers.

"Call it the ballroom," Lindsay suggested. "The polished oak would make a good dance floor, and you may end up liking it so well you leave it this way."

"I'll think about it. Dave Jonas is already here, by the way, waiting impatiently for you. I thought maybe you'd come together."

"You know better than that, Kathy. In this town, three dates and everybody starts watching the mail for a wedding invitation."

Kathy shrugged. "It wouldn't be the end of the world if you married him, you know. He's a nice guy."

"Remember? I tried marriage once."

"It's not Dave's fault that Gibb was impossible. And just because he works on the assembly line at your dad's plant doesn't make him ineligible, either."

Lindsay was startled. "You don't really think I'm petty enough to hold out for some kind of executive, do you, Kathy?"

"No, but—" The bell rang again, and Kathy turned to the door. "Make yourself at home, darling. There's a buffet set up in the dining room, and the bar's in the kitchen. Last time I saw Dave he was on the sun porch."

Lindsay turned thoughtfully toward the dining room. She knew Elmwood too well to have trouble completing Kathy's sentence. *No, but there's been some talk,* she'd been about to say. Because Lindsay had dated Dave Jonas a couple of times and then cooled off the relationship, the gossips were saying she thought she was too good for a mere assembly-line worker.

She sighed. She'd long ago accepted the gossip as the price of staying in Elmwood. Let them think what they liked.

Dave Jonas wasn't on the porch but in the dining room, morosely sampling Swedish meatballs directly from the chafing dish. He looked up with a halfhearted smile when Lindsay greeted him.

She picked up a plate. "You don't look very happy."

He looked over her shoulder. "Are you alone?"

"Yes. Did you think I turned down your invitation so I could come with someone else?"

"Not exactly. I thought you might have your ex along."

"Gibb is not only my ex," Lindsay said deliberately, "he's ancient history. Gone. Kaput. Finished."

Dave didn't look appeased. "Well, that's got some of us worried."

Lindsay frowned. "I don't understand what you mean."

"Oh, it's nothing about you, exactly. But he's got no reason to feel friendly about this plant, does he? It's common knowledge your dad paid him off to get him out of here when you divorced him. So why should he put himself on the line to try to save our jobs?"

"Because it's *his* job that will be on the line if he doesn't. I understand the people at Triangle don't take kindly to failure."

Dave shrugged. "We'll see what happens, I guess."

Lindsay spooned potato salad onto her plate. "Well, try to stay cheerful in the meantime," she advised. "It'd be a shame to waste all that worry."

His smile was more genuine this time. "I'll keep it in mind. Do you really want to eat right now, or shall we go dance?"

Almost an hour later, Lindsay was at the stereo, helping to choose the next round of dance music, when a sudden stillness seemed to drop over the living room. It lasted only a moment, but it was enough to make her turn and look toward the front door.

Skye Oliver was standing there, giving her long dark hair a shake and saying, "I just knew you wouldn't mind if I brought him along, Kathy." Behind her, a man turned from the closet where he'd obviously been hanging up Skye's coat, and she took his arm.

Lindsay supposed she shouldn't have been surprised to see him. Even Gibb needed some recreation now and then, she thought philosophically.

Skye's voice carried easily over the crowd. "After all, poor Gibb knows hardly anyone in Elmwood any more, and as I was telling him over dinner—the lobster at the Willows was wonderful tonight, by the way. Anyway, as

I was telling him, the best place to meet people will be at Kathy Russell's party. And I knew in a crowd like this, you'd never notice one more, Kathy.'' She patted Gibb's sleeve. ''Not that you're easy to overlook, of course, Gibb. But Kathy does have the biggest parties in town. Everyone who's anyone in Elmwood is here.''

''Sometimes,'' Dave Jonas muttered into Lindsay's ear, ''I think it's a wonder that woman doesn't get tangled up and forget what she means to say, herself.''

Lindsay didn't comment. Privately, she thought that Skye's dizzy commentary had not only been well planned but had had precisely the effect the woman intended. A full-page ad in the local newspaper announcing that Skye Oliver was laying claim to Gibb Gardner couldn't have done a more efficient job at spreading the word.

At Lindsay's elbow, Ian Russell muttered, ''Somebody ought to warn the poor sap that in Elmwood, taking a woman out for lobster at the Willows is like buying her a promise ring. Next thing he knows, he'll be shopping for a full-fledged diamond.''

Lindsay choked on a giggle. ''Is that how Kathy hooked you?'' she murmured.

Skye beamed impartially at everyone in her vicinity. Her eyes were bright and her cheeks were a delicate pink from the cold. Or possibly, Lindsay speculated, from whatever she'd been doing just before she and Gibb arrived at the party.

Lindsay slid her hand into the crook of Dave's arm. ''Come on,'' she urged. ''Let's get this music picked out and get the party going again.''

She did her best to keep her distance from Gibb and Skye, but big as the Russells' house was, she couldn't avoid them entirely. She kept hearing Skye's tinkling laugh and bits of her conversation. Gibb, on the other hand, seemed to have very little to say—but every time Lindsay glanced his way he was watching Skye with what appeared to be approval. No wonder the woman was acting as if she was basking in radiant sunlight, Lindsay thought.

Lindsay was directly across the buffet table from the pair when someone asked Skye if it was true that her parents were selling their apartment on the square.

"Heavens, no," Skye said. "I'm not surprised the rumor's started, but they love their little loft, and they wouldn't dream of giving it up. But they're going all the way around the world, you know, so when Gibb came to town and couldn't find anything suitable, I tracked Mama and Papa down in Singapore, and they agreed to sublease it for a few months."

Lindsay's hand froze on the coleslaw spoon. It made no difference where he lived, she told herself firmly. But she couldn't quite convince herself that it didn't matter.

She'd been in the Olivers' apartment once, and she knew the sort of view it commanded of Potpourri and her living room windows. Was that why Gibb had found it so attractive?

"It's so difficult to find living quarters suitable for an executive, you know," Skye was bubbling on. "There are houses, of course. It's really too bad you won't be staying, Gibb."

Lindsay couldn't help it. She murmured, "I'm sure Skye will do her best to find a way."

Skye met Lindsay's gaze and said coolly, "Oh, hello there, Lindsay. Seeing you reminds me that Gibb really should join the Courthouse Squares. Take care of it for me, won't you?"

She'd made it sound almost as if Lindsay was her personal secretary. "I'd be happy to," Lindsay said, with only a hint of irony. "If Gibb likes, of course."

"What are the Courthouse Squares?" he asked warily. "It sounds like a dance club."

He was looking at Lindsay, but Skye laughed and put her hand on his sleeve. "It's just a silly little social organization, Gibb. A dead bore to belong to, actually, but it's expected."

"All the people who have apartments above the shops around the square are members," Lindsay said deliberately. "I'm the president this year."

She was watching Gibb's face, and she didn't miss the sudden narrowing of his eyes. "Then you live on the square, too?"

"Above my shop." She felt relieved, and a little silly, all at the same time. Of course he hadn't taken the Olivers' apartment so he could spy on her, because he hadn't even known she lived there.

"I don't think I'll have much time for socializing," Gibb said.

It was exactly the response Lindsay had anticipated. "What a pity," she murmured. "I'm sure Skye's disappointed to hear that." *But I'm not*, her tone of voice said.

Gibb caught the unstated message, Lindsay was certain, because the corner of his mouth quirked just a little. "Still," he murmured, "as I was going to say before I was interrupted, perhaps I'd enjoy being a Courthouse Square. Sign me up, won't you, Lindsay?"

She supposed she ought to have known Gibb couldn't turn down a challenge like the one she'd tossed at him. She shouldn't have given in to the impulse to bait him. Not that it made much difference, really. She doubted he'd take any part in the social life of the Courthouse Squares. And even if he did, he'd soon learn that Skye was right about one thing, at least—it wasn't the liveliest of organizations.

But Lindsay was uneasy, nevertheless, as she remembered the way his eyes had narrowed when she'd told him where she lived. Had it been simple masculine ego that had inspired his about-face? Or was there something more going on?

Of course not, she told herself firmly. She was being slightly paranoid, that was all. Gibb didn't give a darn where she lived or what she did—and that was just fine with Lindsay.

CHAPTER FOUR

LINDSAY added a little broth to the pan in which her pot roast was simmering and rearranged the potatoes and carrots around the meat so they'd cook more evenly. It was a man-size meal, the kind she seldom cooked except for Sunday lunch, when her father often came to eat with them.

She glanced at the clock and called, "Beep, come and set the table. Your grandpa will be here any minute."

"Oh, Mom, there's lots of time yet. And I'm winning—I'm in line for a big prize."

Lindsay didn't doubt that; even from the next room she could hear the steady chirps coming from the computer's speakers as Beep racked up points on the game Ben Armentrout had given him for Christmas. "You can say that again, sweetheart. You've got three minutes to get started on the table, or the prize you'll win is an entire week without computer games."

Seconds short of the deadline, Beep appeared in the kitchen with the big black cat draped around his neck. "A whole week? You wouldn't really do that, would you, Mom?"

"Put Spats down and get to work or you'll find out," Lindsay recommended. "And wash your hands before you start."

Beep made a face. "Cats are cleaner than most humans," he argued. "It says so in one of my books."

"I don't doubt it. Nevertheless, we have house rules around here—remember?"

59

Beep picked up his kite from the table and hung it on a hook beside the back door. "I wonder what Gibb will be doing this afternoon."

Lindsay got a head of lettuce from the refrigerator. "Probably catching up on all the work he wasn't doing last night."

"Last night? At the party, you mean? Did you see him?"

Lindsay could have bitten her tongue off. "He was there, yes," she said reluctantly.

"Oh. He said he had a date, but he didn't say he was going to the party. He told me about it 'cause he couldn't stay and fly the kite longer." Beep pulled a stool over to the cabinet and selected three plates. "Was she pretty? I think he deserves somebody who's pretty."

"He certainly deserves her," Lindsay said under her breath. Then she caught herself. This might be an unexpected opportunity to bring Beep back in touch with reality without shattering his self-esteem. If he thought Gibb had found a love interest, surely he would realize that he couldn't count on a repetition of yesterday's fun. "She was very pretty, and he seemed quite taken with her. In fact, I wouldn't be surprised if he spends a lot of his free time with her from now on."

"Oh." Beep's voice was rather small.

Lindsay's heart twisted a little, and she had to remind herself that she wasn't exaggerating in the least. Skye *was* attractive, at least to people with a taste for tall, almost-anorexic brunettes. Gibb had seemed perfectly content to stay by her side last night. And Lindsay wouldn't mind betting a considerable sum that they'd see a lot more of each other in the near future—especially if Skye had anything to say about it.

Besides, she reflected, sometimes a small hurt up front could save a big smash later. It was sort of like giving Beep his shots when he was a baby—the prick of the needle had made him scream for a minute, but the illness the vaccination prevented would have been far worse.

If only it was as easy to inoculate him against the kind of wounds a careless adult could inflict.

Ben Armentrout stamped up the stairs. "It sure smells good in here," he called from the door. "Have I already done something wonderful to deserve it, or is there a request coming up?"

Lindsay laughed. "Well, since you mentioned it—we do have a leaky bathroom faucet."

"Say no more." He inhaled deeply. "Feed me like this, and I'll give you a whole new bathroom, my dear."

"I'll settle for getting the faulty washer replaced."

Beep tossed flatware onto the table in a heap and rushed to give Ben a hug. "It's been an awful long time since I saw you, Grandpa."

"I've been working hard at the plant this week, my boy."

Beep nodded wisely. "With Gibb. He told me about it yesterday while we were building my new kite."

Ben shot a look at Lindsay, his eyebrows raised.

She shook her head. "Don't ask me what's going on, Daddy. I heard about the kite, but not the rest."

"Well, it sounds like Beep's heard more than Gibb's been telling me," Ben said in an undertone. He looked speculatively at his grandson and added, "Let's you and I go tear up a faucet, young man, and you can tell me all about it."

Lindsay arranged the salad greens on crystal plates and sliced a loaf of French bread. From the bathroom she could hear the murmur of voices, Beep's high-pitched childish tones mixing with Ben's baritone, but she couldn't make out the words.

She checked the vegetables and finished setting the table. She and Beep needed to have a discussion about leaving his chores undone, she decided, but she'd wait till Ben had gone. He was quite capable of siding with Beep to tell Lindsay she was expecting too much, and it was difficult enough to discipline an eight-year-old without having to take on her father, as well.

When she went to call them to dinner, Beep was walking back and forth along the edge of the bathtub as if it was a balance beam, flailing his arms theatrically. Ben had extracted a flimsy rubber washer from the faucet and was drying it on one of her best white towels. Lindsay winced.

"There's always chocolates," Beep said earnestly.

"And flowers," Ben suggested. "Roses, maybe."

Beep shook his head and almost lost his balance. "But, Grandpa—"

Lindsay leaned against the bathroom door. "Just who are we buying chocolates and flowers for? Has one of you acquired a girlfriend I should know about?"

"Only you," Ben said. "And our favorite girl has a birthday coming up next month, remember?"

"Don't remind me, Daddy."

"What do you want for your birthday, Mom?"

She hugged Beep. Standing on the bathtub edge, he was almost as tall as she was, and Lindsay had a mental flash of a future day when he'd be all grown up and probably have to bend over to give her a hug. It scared her a little to think how soon that day would come, and she had to clear her throat before she could say, "Not a thing, honey. I've got you, and that's the best present of all. Now wash up while I get the pot roast out of the pan.''

Beep gave her a cheeky grin. ''We can't. You told us to take the faucet apart, and now the sink won't work.''

Lindsay ruffled his hair and threatened lightly, ''I could always take you out back in the courtyard, hook up the garden hose and scrub you from head to foot.''

Beep squealed with mock fear and ran for the kitchen with Lindsay in pursuit. Ben followed, shaking his head.

The pot roast won approval all around, though Beep spent more time talking than eating. Gibb figured large in his conversation, and from time to time Lindsay felt her father's gaze resting speculatively on her. But Ben didn't say anything till after dessert, when Beep asked to be excused to return to his games.

As soon as the computer started chirping once more, Lindsay poured her father a second cup of coffee and sat down across from him.

''He's got a serious case, doesn't he?'' Ben said.

Lindsay nodded. ''Did Gibb really tell Beep about the plant?''

''As far as I can figure out, he didn't say anything that isn't common knowledge. Mostly Beep was telling me about a movie he and the baby-sitter saw on television last night.''

''One I wouldn't have let him watch, no doubt.''

''Of course you wouldn't. It seems to have been one car chase after another, with a couple of kidnappings thrown in for good measure. Lindsay, what are you going to do?''

She didn't pretend to misunderstand. ''About the hero worship? I don't know. I'll have to talk to Gibb, I suppose. The problem is that all he did, really, was replace a kite he stepped on. It was no big deal to him—

it wouldn't be to any adult. But he's got no idea how little it takes to make someone a hero to an eight-year-old."

"Or a goat, when the idol turns out to have clay feet."

Lindsay sighed. "And I'm afraid Beep will find out, as I did, that Gibb's clay feet go all the way to the neck."

Ben sipped his coffee. "I'll have to drive out to the hardware store to get a new washer. Want me to take Beep along?"

"So I can slip off and talk to Gibb?" Lindsay considered. "That might be better than seeing him at the office. Thanks, Daddy."

Too soon, it seemed to Lindsay, Ben finished his coffee and talked Beep into leaving the computer to go to the store. "Can I look in the toy department, too?" Beep asked as they were going out the door.

Lindsay called, almost automatically, "He doesn't need anything, Daddy."

Ben didn't answer, just waved a dismissing hand.

Lindsay dawdled over straightening up the kitchen and finally had to force herself to cross the square and climb the stairs to the Olivers' apartment.

Gibb's gesture had been such a simple one, but trying to explain the effect it had on Beep was going to be far more complicated. Gibb probably had no idea of the chain reaction he'd set off, and whatever Lindsay said, she'd probably end up sounding like an overprotective mom, a fool who was trying to shield her child from shadows.

She rang the bell and heard nothing. She'd just decided with a sigh of relief that Gibb must not be at home when the door opened silently.

He seemed even taller in a casual ski sweater that emphasized the breadth of his shoulders. He didn't speak, just looked at her with a half-question in his eyes.

Lindsay was finding it hard to get her breath. There was something about the way he was looking at her that was disconcerting, and she tried without success to figure out what it was. It wasn't tension, exactly—at least, he didn't seem to be under a strain or to feel irritated at seeing her. But it felt as if there was a coiled spring inside him—a powerful force that had been drawn up and compressed and was just waiting for a careless word or action to release the energy.

His eyebrows rose.

"I'm sorry to bother you," she managed to say. "But may I have a few minutes?"

"Of course." He stepped back from the door. "Would you like coffee? Or maybe a glass of wine? I can't offer you much, I'm afraid—the pantry's a bit bare."

"Coffee would be fine."

She paused on the Oriental rug that set off the foyer area and looked around. Originally the upper level of the commercial buildings around the square had been warrens of storerooms and tiny, airless, low-rent apartments. The renovation had knocked out almost all the walls and created a vast, high-ceilinged space that could be adapted in a hundred ways. The Olivers' apartment, much like Lindsay's, was laid out on an open plan, with one enormous room—a combination living space, dining room and kitchen—stretching almost the full length of the building and a narrow hallway off to the side that led to private bedrooms and baths.

The basic floor plan was where the resemblance ended, however; Lindsay's apartment tended toward the homey and comfortable, while the Olivers' could have appeared in any decorating magazine.

"I can't believe they rented this to you," she said.

From the island kitchen toward the back of the big open room, Gibb said, "Not everyone thinks of me in the same category with ax murderers, Lindsay."

"I didn't mean anything personal. It's obvious that Skye thinks you're wonderful, but still—" Lindsay bit her tongue. What a great way to start, she thought ironically, and tried again. "It's just that there are antiques here that belong in museums, so I can't imagine why they'd rent it to anyone."

Gibb looked at her thoughtfully for a moment and then finished scooping coffee into a filter. "Did you come over here to warn me about Skye?"

"No, I didn't."

"Well, that's good."

"I have no interest in any woman you might be seeing."

"Of course you don't," he murmured.

The words were reassuring, but the tone wasn't, and Lindsay was annoyed. Did he honestly think she was jealous? Surely not; Gibb wasn't a fool. "You sound just a little doubtful. Why? Has Skye been speculating that I might try to get you back?"

"Are you considering it?"

"Don't be ridiculous. But it's the sort of thing Skye would say in order to manipulate you into spending time with her. If she made it sound as if she was protecting you from the big, bad ex-wife..."

He smiled. "Are you afraid I won't recognize the technique, Lindsay?"

"It's none of my business what you do. But I'd suggest, in your own best interests, that you be cautious."

"You don't need to worry about that. You see, I remember when you used something very similar on me."

Lindsay was stunned. "I did not!"

"You certainly did. The moment I walked into your father's office, on the very first day you worked there, you started spinning webs for me. If that's the way you'd been behaving at that fancy college of yours, I'd say it's no wonder they kicked you out."

"I wasn't expelled, Gibb. My grades were just a little low, that's all."

"Oh, is that why Ben brought you home and put you to work where he could keep an eye on you?" Gibb sounded unconvinced. "I learned from the experience, of course. I think there must be something very charming about a female black widow spider, too—or else those unfortunate males wouldn't fall into the mating trap. I was lucky enough to escape with my life, and I don't plan to make the same mistake twice."

"Well, hurrah for you," Lindsay said coolly. Her pride was prickling a little. Did he really need to make it sound as if being married to her had been like a close brush with death?

He poured two cups of coffee and brought one over to her. "If you aren't here to undermine Skye, then perhaps you came to collect my dues?" He indicated a pair of velvet-covered chairs near the fireplace.

Lindsay took one. "Dues? For the Courthouse Squares, you mean? I think we can make it an honorary membership—after all, the Olivers have already paid once."

"Oh, I wouldn't want you to give me special treatment."

"In that case, you can pay me ten dollars and I'll see that you get a membership card," Lindsay said irritably.

Gibb pulled out his wallet. "How long have you lived on the square?"

"Since I started the shop."

"And when was that?"

"When Beep was about a year old. Daddy sold the house then, and I decided it was time for a fresh start."

"You'd been working for Ben up till then?"

She looked at him levelly over the rim of her cup. "I'm not applying for a job, Gibb, and I haven't agreed to a game of twenty questions—so I don't think I need to tell you all this."

He shrugged. "I'm just curious. Something's certainly changed you."

"I don't see why you'd think it's any of your business—but in case you're really interested, it's Beep that's made all the difference in my life."

"Well, I'm glad it's all worked out so well for you." His tone was dismissive. "You have everything you wanted."

"He's a very special little boy." She took a deep breath. "That's why I came, Gibb. I want to talk to you about Beep." She fiddled with her cup for a moment while the silence lengthened, trying to find a way to start. "I hope he thanked you properly for the kite."

"Yes, he did. Is that what this is about, Lindsay? I'm in trouble for buying your kid a kite?"

"Not exactly. It was very thoughtful. But I need to ask about your intentions."

His eyebrows soared. "My *what*? Is there any reason on earth I should have intentions where Benjamin's concerned?"

"Of course not," Lindsay said sharply. "I've already made that clear—you've got nothing to do with his life."

"Precisely. So will you tell me what the hell this is about? It was only a kite, Lindsay."

"I know this sounds petty, but it's not the kite that's the problem, Gibb. It's the attention." She took a deep breath. "You see, Beep's fascinated with you. You're a stranger, and that makes you exotic—unique. And you paid attention to him, which makes you special. And I'm afraid he's expecting it to continue."

"Perhaps you should stop reading fairy tales to him," Gibb said dryly.

Lindsay set her cup aside. "I should have known you wouldn't understand," she said quietly. "Thanks for the coffee. I won't keep you from your work any longer."

Silently, he followed her to the door.

With one hand on the knob, Lindsay turned toward him, but she didn't even try to meet his gaze. "Please, Gibb, don't let him count on you."

"That's the last thing I'd want to happen. All I want to do is get my work finished and get on to the next job."

"You know that, and I know that. But Beep doesn't understand that you don't believe in being tied down. Living right here—you're apt to keep on seeing him now and then. Please don't let him get his hopes up."

He didn't answer, and Lindsay walked across the square with her shoulders slumped, feeling that the whole exercise had been a waste of time. She had accomplished nothing.

Except, of course, she realized gloomily, she had accidentally told Gibb precisely how to hurt her, if he was so inclined. All he had to do was seek out Beep.

Gibb stood by the window and watched her walk across the square. She was almost to the door of Potpourri when a car pulled up in front, and Ben Armentrout and her son got out. The child was clutching a large, bright-colored box. The three of them vanished inside the building, and Gibb sat down at the table where he'd spread out a set of reports for study.

But he didn't look at the papers. He was still seeing Lindsay's face—lovely, troubled, full of tenderness as she talked about her son.

She had smelled, very faintly, of strawberries. The unexpectedness of the scent haunted him. In the old days she had preferred Midnight Passion at several hundred dollars an ounce. He'd never forget the row they'd had the time he'd gotten a credit-card bill for two ounces in one month.

But now she smelled of out-of-season strawberries, and somehow that unexpected aroma was more sensual than any amount of musk could ever be. He'd had to move away from the soft, caressing fragrance of her, and even at a distance it had stayed with him, as if her scent had lodged in his brain.

He hadn't noticed it at the party last night, or inside Potpourri. But the gift shop was full of smells, and the women at the party had been drenched in a variety of perfumes. And even at the Willows on Friday when he'd bent to kiss her cheek, Gibb hadn't smelled strawberries. All he'd noticed then was the softness of her skin.

Kissing her had been a foolish stunt. She'd annoyed him with her acid remark about how little she wanted to see him, and he'd taken the easiest and quickest route to get even, by embarrassing her in front of a crowd.

He hadn't expected it to affect him—but the action had backfired. Perhaps he'd thought that she'd be wizened, her skin dry and hard to the touch. But her cheek had been like velvet against his lips, as soft and yielding as she had once been in their marriage bed.

Today, when they'd been alone together in private for the first time, he'd had to exert restraint to keep from touching her again. The effort had made him prickly— which hadn't been so bad, after all, since it had sent her away before his self-control eroded.

Lindsay had told him once in the heat of anger that he had no business being married. The indictment had been no surprise to Gibb. He'd known for years that he wasn't a good prospect as a husband, and he'd always intended never to marry. Until Lindsay came along and blindsided him with her loveliness—and for a while he'd thought it was possible to work it out after all.

But she'd been right; he wasn't a marriageable sort of man. He never had been, and he never would be. Besides, even though he hadn't changed over the last nine years, Lindsay had. She had her child now, and Benjamin was the center of her universe. What had happened between her and Gibb was over. Done.

It was crazy for him to still want her, in any way at all.

Beep sat cross-legged on the polished oak floor of their apartment, racing the remote-control car Ben had bought him that afternoon. It was a super-deluxe, high-powered model, doubtless the most expensive on the market— but they'd both looked so pleased when they came home from the hardware store with it that Lindsay hadn't had the heart to object. In fact, by the end of the afternoon she hadn't been sure who was enjoying it more—the little boy or the old man.

In any case, the focus of her thoughts had been elsewhere. She couldn't forget what Gibb had said about her pursuing him—even though she hadn't done any such thing.

She'd been barely nineteen, and her first few months away from home at college had seemed a frolic—until her grades came back looking pathetic, and Ben Armentrout had swooped down on her dormitory room and informed his errant daughter that he wasn't paying her tuition in order for her to be a social butterfly.

When Lindsay had pleaded for a second chance, he'd wavered, then said no. A semester at home, doing the sort of work that was all she could expect to find without an education, might reinforce the lesson, he decreed, and perhaps it would send her back to college the following year determined to study instead of party.

Lindsay had cried and pouted all the way to Elmwood. Because he ordered her to, she reported for work at the Armentrout plant on the following Monday morning, to take up the secretarial post Ben had created for her in his office—but she was an hour late, filled with resentment and determined to make her father as miserable as she was.

But first thing that morning Ben had told her cheerfully that she'd be working for his new assistant instead, and he'd called Gibb in and suggested blandly that if Lindsay didn't perform up to standards, a spanking might be more effective than the more common means of employee discipline.

Lindsay had taken one look at Gibb—tall, dark, lean, handsome, far-too-serious Gibb—and decided that working at the plant might not be a fate worse than death, after all.

Her first resolution was that she'd get him to smile at her before the day was out. If she'd succeeded, that might have been the end of it. But it was the better part of a week before she managed the feat—and by then she was hooked on Gibbson Gardner. She even knew the sound of his step in the corridor, and whenever he spoke to her, she had to concentrate on every word to avoid losing herself in the rich huskiness of his voice. And she would have done anything to bring that fleeting smile to his face, and the softness to his eyes....

She felt color rise to her cheeks, and admitted that Gibb's accusation this afternoon had been absolutely correct. She *had* laid traps for him—such subtle ones that half the time she hadn't been aware herself what she was doing.

It had taken her a month to get him to ask her to a movie. And as long as she was being honest, she had to confess that she'd been the one to initiate their first kiss, too—when he'd taken her home afterward—though she'd been very careful to make it seem like an accident.

But the kisses that came after that first tentative brush of the lips hadn't been her doing; once the ice was broken, it was Gibb who'd taken charge, and who had eventually taught her what passion meant.

Beep giggled. "Look, Mom, Spats is chasing my car!" He backed the vehicle up and raced it off in a new direction, with the big black cat leaping in pursuit. "He's acting like a dog!"

Lindsay's gaze rested almost unseeingly on her son. She could sympathize with Beep's attraction to Gibb, and she could understand Skye's fascination with him, too—for Lindsay had felt it all herself. There was something about that almost-somber attitude of Gibb's that made him seem incredibly sad, even haunted—and made others want to add a relieving sparkle to his life.

What had caused that sadness, Lindsay had never known. Gibb hadn't told her much about his past—and in truth, she hadn't asked. She'd been very young, and anything outside the reality of the present didn't seem to matter. Secure in her own ability to fascinate him, she'd been convinced they'd have a perfect life together. Certainly the dim and distant past couldn't affect their future happiness. They had almost everything—an insatiable passion for each other, a dollhouse of an apartment, even a financially secure future, for Ben Armentrout would make sure of that.

The only thing lacking to make Lindsay's happiness complete was a baby. But Gibb had refused to consider the possibility of a child. He had refused even to discuss the matter—he had simply announced that he didn't care for children and didn't plan to have any. Lindsay had accused him of selfishness, Gibb had gone silent—and that was when the fights had started. The quarrels were always about something else, however, for he had won that round, and they no longer talked about a child.

But not speaking of the baby she wanted so badly didn't make Lindsay's longing go away. If anything, the craving grew stronger as she nursed it silently in her heart. The fights went on, and each one left their marriage a little more tattered, until finally Lindsay had faced the fact that there was nothing left and brought the pretense to an end.

But though she knew she had done the only thing she could, the breakup of her storybook romance had sent her into a tailspin. She had done some things she wasn't proud of in the months after Gibb had left—some very stupid things. And she had never gone back to school, of course, for by the time she could, there had been Beep to think of....

"It's bedtime," she announced.

"Oh, Mom..." But the protest was no more than automatic; Beep parked his remote-control car neatly under the coffee table and padded off to his room.

He wasn't perfect, of course—Beep could be as stubborn and willful as Lindsay had once been. He dawdled over his chores, he argued about what he should be allowed to do, and he possessed a particular high-pitched giggle that affected Lindsay exactly the same way as did fingernails scraping on a blackboard.

But he was a good child—and he had been her salvation. She had wanted him so badly that she had pulled herself back from the brink. And at the moment when, still exhausted from her labor, she first held him in her arms, she had fallen instantly in love—and she had resolved that she would never fail this tiny human being who was now depending on her for everything.

Beep was already in bed, with the cat curled up at his feet. As she came in, Lindsay saw him slide something under his pillow, so as she stooped to kiss him, she reached under the pillow and tugged out a comic book and a pen-size flashlight.

She looked from the contraband to Beep, who was studying her as if he was trying to figure out what sort of explanation she might fall for. "I think we've talked before about reading under the blankets after bedtime, Beep," she murmured. "And as for the subject matter you've chosen..." She studied the garish cover of the comic book and wrinkled her nose. "You know how I feel about violence, whether it's in cartoons or movies or comic books."

"But this is the Crime Stompers, Mom. They're the *good* guys."

"Tell you what," Lindsay said. "I'll take this out to the living room and read it, and if I approve you can have it back tomorrow."

Beep sighed. "Just don't throw it away, all right?"

She feigned surprise. "What's this? You sound as if you think I won't like it!"

"I'm not an idiot, Mom. But it's not mine, okay? I borrowed it from Josh."

"In that case, I'll return it to his mother," Lindsay said crisply. She tucked the comforter around him and kissed his forehead again. "Sleep tight, honey. Want me to leave Spats in or take him out?"

"In," Beep said, and yawned as she shut off the lights.

It was the loneliest time of day. The apartment was quiet, though now and then the building creaked as old buildings will. The courthouse was dark, except for the moonlight gleaming on the windows and the polished brass hands of the big clock in the tower.

Across the corner of the square, in the Olivers' apartment, the lights burned brightly, and she could see a silhouette bent over a table beyond an undraped window.

Gibb was working late, she thought. It wasn't any surprise; he'd said this afternoon that he was anxious to have this job done and shake the dust of Elmwood off his feet once more.

Well, he couldn't be more impatient than she was. The day Gibb left, Lindsay would dance all the way around the square.

CHAPTER FIVE

THE problems at the Armentrout plant were not going to be easily solved, and the difficult decisions that must be made absorbed much of Gibb's attention over the next few days. On Tuesday afternoon he left work early and went to the apartment to make a few very private phone calls. There was no point in upsetting Ben Armentrout or getting his hopes raised until Gibb had something concrete to tell him. Then, once his phone calls were finished, he intended to put his feet up and contemplate the future of Ben's business. In the silence of the apartment, he could better assess the possibilities than he could in the confusion of the plant itself.

Instead, he found himself thinking of Lindsay. It was purely imagination, of course, to think that he could still smell her fragrance in the apartment. And it was insane to let himself remember the passions they had once shared, instead of the ones that had driven them apart.

But he couldn't keep himself from thinking of the way she had always been able to set his blood on fire with a touch. Of course, that same fire had burned up any common sense he'd ever possessed, as well.

The sexual attraction that had flared between them—intense and powerful though it was—hadn't been nearly enough to outweigh their problems nine years ago. And even though he couldn't deny that he still felt the remnants of that attraction now, he'd better not let himself forget that there was a world of difference between physical desire and the kind of feelings it took to make a marriage work—the kind of feelings that were so far beyond him.

Wanting her was one thing—foolish, yes, but understandable. The softness of her skin, the gleam of her hair, the brilliance of her eyes—all he had to do was look at her, and he couldn't help but remember what it had been like to lie in her arms.

The doorbell rang. For an instant, he didn't even recognize the sound, for he'd been so far away.

He considered not answering the door. If someone at Triangle or the Armentrout plant needed him, they'd have phoned, and nobody else had a reason to seek him out.

But a couple of minutes later the bell rang again, longer and more persistently. Gibb swore under his breath as he went to open the door. Probably some religious missionary or door-to-door salesman, and he'd soon send them off with a flea in the ear. Didn't people realize just because someone was at home didn't mean he was free?

Lindsay's son was standing on the mat, his golden-blond hair almost hidden under a too-big baseball cap, a backpack slung over one shoulder, grinning cheerfully. "Hi, Gibb. I saw your car out back."

So this was what Lindsay had been talking about on Sunday, Gibb reflected. Because of that silly business with the kite, the kid had concluded Gibb was his own personal playmate.

Well, he thought philosophically, in a sense he'd asked for it. It just showed what happened when you broke the habits of years and violated a sane and reasonable rule to have nothing to do with children—you ended up with young Benjamin Gardner standing on the welcome mat, displaying an eager grin.

The grin had faded a little, however, Gibb noted. The kid was obviously no dummy; he'd realized already that he wasn't exactly welcome. Gibb told himself he ought to feel glad of it, because it made his task easier. All he had to do was gruffly tell the child it wasn't a good time to visit, and that would be the end of it.

But he couldn't, because he recognized the look in the boy's eyes. If it had been anger or frustration, Gibb could have stood it. Though those feelings might have been unjust, they would have been directed outward, at Gibb—and he was plenty big enough to take it. He was used to it; nobody got to where he had in the world without learning that one couldn't be admired all the time.

But what he saw in the wide-set brown eyes was pain and self-doubt. The child not only sensed a rejection coming, but he was already wondering which short-comings of his own had brought it on. And Gibb, who hadn't forgotten what it was like to meet with rejection and the feelings of inadequacy it raised, couldn't let the kid think it was his own fault.

Please don't let him get his hopes up, Lindsay had said. But it was obviously already too late for that. He'd have to try to let him down gently.

Gibb's voice was gruff. "So you came to entertain me? That's very thoughtful, but—"

Beep shook his head. "No. I came to ask you a question—sort of a favor, really. It'll just take a minute, but I can't come back later, you see."

"Because you don't want your mother to know you're here," Gibb concluded.

"It's a secret. She won't miss me right now, because usually I have soccer practice after school, but the coach was sick today. So I came home early and saw your car. Can I come in?"

He already *was* in, Gibb realized; somehow the kid had wriggled around him and into the foyer. He shrugged. "For a few minutes, but I have work to do."

"I won't take long." The child marched across the Olivers' living room and climbed up on the couch. It was bigger and deeper than it looked, and it almost swallowed him.

Gibb pulled a straight-backed chair around and straddled it. "I don't know how your mother would feel about you and me having secrets, pal."

"But it's a nice secret," Beep assured him. "It isn't the kind that could hurt anybody."

Gibb wasn't so certain about that, but he supposed that he was in for it now. He guessed he'd just have to listen, decline to comment, and then put the kid out the door the same way he'd expel a troublesome insect.

The doorbell rang. This time two heads turned toward the foyer with disbelief, and Gibb's eyes narrowed as he once more focused on the child. "If that's your mother, we're both going to be in the sauce."

"I don't think anybody would tell her the coach was sick." Beep added helpfully, "But just in case, shall I hide?"

"No! The last thing I need is for her to find you hiding in my apartment."

"Oh. I was watching a movie once where this guy hid in a girl's closet when her boyfriend came by so they wouldn't get in trouble. It sounded like a really good idea, but he was too big to fit and the boyfriend almost found him anyway, so he had to go out the window instead but he had hardly any clothes on and—''

Gibb paused halfway across the living room. "I don't suppose your mother knew you were watching this movie?"

The child shook his head. "Why did he have hardly any clothes on, anyway?"

"You're terrifying," Gibb said under his breath, and opened the door a crack.

Skye smiled at him and stood on tiptoe to kiss his cheek. "Hello, Gibb, dear. I hoped you'd be home. Mother called today from Kuala Lumpur—can you believe it?—and wanted me to express her a couple of sweaters. I guess they're going up into the mountains and..." She looked over his shoulder. "Oh, do you have company? I heard voices but I thought it was just the television." She saw Beep, and her eyes widened. "What's *he* doing here?"

"Trying to sell me something for a school project, I suspect," Gibb said dryly. "We were just getting to the point when you came."

"Oh. For a moment there I actually wondered..." Her voice trailed off.

If I think he's my son, Gibb thought. "No. I have it on the best authority."

"Well, I'm glad Lindsay isn't trying to pull anything over on you." She advanced on Beep, her hand held out. "Hello, there, young man."

With an effort, the child pushed himself up from the depths of the couch to stand and shake her hand. "Good afternoon, Miss Oliver."

"Gracious—the child has manners! I won't keep you both from your business, I'll just run and get Mother's sweaters."

When she came back from the bedroom wing with a shopping bag, Skye paused beside Gibb and said softly, "Shall I get some steaks to cook tonight?"

He shook his head. "Not for me. I have a lot of work, Skye."

She pouted, prettily. "You have to eat sometime." But she didn't press the issue.

Gibb closed the door behind her.

"Is that the girl you took to the party?" Beep had perched on the very edge of the couch. "*I* don't think she's awfully pretty."

"I don't recall anyone asking you," Gibb said mildly.

"Oh. I'm sorry if it's none of my business. It's just that Mom said you like her a lot because she's really pretty, but I don't think—"

"Did she, now?" Gibb sat down. "Why don't you tell me what this visit is all about, Benjamin?"

"Okay. The secret is that it's Mom's birthday soon."

"April fifteenth," Gibb agreed.

"You know when her birthday is?"

"I'll never forget it. She was born on the same day income tax is due and the *Titanic* sank."

Beep's eyes were huge. "I don't understand."

"Good. What about the birthday? If you want to have a party, I'm sorry, but I have no experience with things like that, so my advice wouldn't be worth much. If—"

"No. I just want to get her a present. A *nice* present. But she has everything already in the shop—all the stuff that girls like. You know, music boxes and bells and wreaths and teddy bears and all that sort of stuff."

"I can see that would create a problem," Gibb agreed.

"Grandpa says you can't ever go wrong with flowers and chocolates, but—"

"With a smart grandpa like that, I don't quite understand why you're talking to me."

Beep heaved an enormous sigh. "Because that's not what I want to get her. I found a necklace at Henderson's Jewelry, but I won't get enough allowance in time. And the next month will be Mother's Day, so I'll have to save up for that, too."

"So it's a matter of money?"

Beep nodded. "I want to earn some more, and I wondered if you'd let me work for you."

This, Gibb thought, had to be the most unusual job interview he'd ever experienced. "Why not work for your grandpa?"

"Because if I ask he'll just give me money instead, and Mom has a fit whenever that happens."

Gibb's eyebrows soared. Lindsay turning down a handout from her father wasn't a picture he could easily imagine.

"I could wash your car," Beep offered.

"On the same day I'm the starting pitcher at Yankee Stadium, maybe."

Beep had to think that over. "Does that mean you won't let me? Mom explained I could have scratched it, sitting on the bumper that way. I'm really sorry."

Gibb said gruffly, "Well, I shouldn't have yelled at you about it." He braced himself to tell the child that there wasn't a single chore he could think of that a kid could do—and that even if he could come up with something, he wouldn't hire him, because Lindsay would probably have him hauled into court for violating the child labor laws if he did.

But he couldn't bring himself to look into those wide, hopeful brown eyes and turn the kid down. He stood up. "Look, Benjamin—give me a chance to consider it.

I'll let you know if I think of anything you can do for me.''

Beep beamed. ''All right!'' He held up a hand for a high-five slap. ''Just remember—this is our secret.''

''Of course.'' He ushered the child out, closed the door and leaned against it. At least he'd bought a little time to find an excuse that the boy would accept.

The last thing he needed was a midget employee whose mother would blow up like a case of dynamite if she heard about the arrangement.

On Friday morning, Beep was already up when Lindsay went into his room to wake him. In fact, he was at the kitchen table, spooning up his cereal with one hand while he traced the mazelike puzzle printed on the back of the breakfast-food box with the other.

Lindsay paused and yawned. ''What hit you this morning?'' she wanted to know.

Beep grinned. ''It's our field trip today.''

Lindsay hadn't forgotten, but she hadn't expected him to be so excited; he'd been visiting the Armentrout plant an average of once a week since he was born. But of course, going on a school bus and showing off his superior knowledge to his classmates would make the trip different and exciting.

''Will Gibb be there, Mom?''

Lindsay's heart sank. Beep had hardly mentioned the man's name all week, and as far as she knew, he hadn't even caught a glimpse of him. She hadn't seen Gibb, either; from the little her father had said, he seemed to be spending all his time absorbed in the plant—which of course, ought to be no surprise to anyone.

She'd actually allowed herself to start thinking not only that her visit on Sunday had had the desired effect on

Gibb, but that Beep didn't really care anyway. She'd begun to believe that she'd been overreacting after all, jumping at shadows.

But now it seemed that Beep had only been biding his time.

"I don't know," she said carelessly. "I suppose so, but I doubt you'll see him on the tour. Your grandpa says he's been pretty busy." She tousled Beep's hair. "Just be on your best behavior, because I'll be keeping an eye on you."

"Are you coming, too?"

"Of course. Lucky me—room mothers get to go on all the trips. This time I don't have to ride the bus, though. I'll just meet you there."

Beep frowned. "But the bus is the best part," he argued.

Better than Gibb? Lindsay wanted to ask, but she wasn't sure she'd like the answer.

She was waiting in her car when the big yellow school bus pulled up in front of the Armentrout plant that afternoon, and she crossed the street from the parking lot to join the seething mass of third-graders as they piled off the bus and formed an untidy line outside the security gates.

Kathy Russell looked frazzled, as well as happy to see Lindsay. "The other room mother stood me up at the last minute," she muttered. "So I'll take the front of the group and let you keep an eye out for stragglers at the back, if that's okay."

Lindsay nodded.

"And I need to talk to you sometime about one of my kids. I just found out that both parents are out of work, and if the Armentrout Trust could help a little..."

"Sure. There isn't much in the fund right now, but Daddy will be writing a check at the end of the month, as soon as the plant's books are balanced. How much do you need?"

"Not a lot—just enough for some shoes and clothes. It's so important at this age for the kids to fit in and not look radically different from their peers." Her voice trailed off as the security gates opened and Ben Armentrout himself came out to greet them.

Lindsay had made the tour a hundred times, with school children, visiting dignitaries, even a vice-president of the United States. She could have guided it herself, though probably not with the verve that Ben Armentrout always displayed. He especially enjoyed the kids—explaining the principles of batteries and quizzing them to see how much they knew about electricity.

Most of the kids were attentive, but she still felt a bit uneasy. There were really too many of them to keep a close eye on every one. Beep, obviously bored with Ben's explanation of precisely how a battery powered a toy, was looking around, and it was only a matter of time before his restlessness communicated itself to the kids around him.

She didn't see Gibb till he was at her elbow. "Ben really gets into this, doesn't he?" he said softly.

Lindsay jumped. There was no reason to feel that he'd sneaked up on her; he had a perfect right to be there. But she couldn't help wondering if part of her uneasy feeling had been because he'd been watching her.

"He's always in his element with the kids," she said. "He even passes out samples at the end of the tour for them to take home."

Ben asked, "Who can tell me why some batteries are called dry cells?"

Hands waved in the air, and Lindsay stopped listening; she'd learned this stuff in her cradle, but to these children it was exciting and new, and they'd be absorbed for a few minutes at least. She turned to Gibb. "I appreciate you leaving Beep alone," she said quietly.

There was a flicker in his eyes, which made her wonder for a moment, but his voice was level. "Don't give me the credit. I've hardly had time to do anything else this week."

"Daddy told me how busy you've been. In fact, I'm surprised you have an hour to spend on a tour."

He shrugged. "I'm not exactly killing time, you know—I'm observing the production process. I just happened to cross paths with the tour."

Beep wriggled through the crowd and appeared at Gibb's side, a smile creasing his face. "Hi, Gibb," he whispered eagerly. "I was hoping I'd see you today!"

Lindsay's gaze clung to Gibb's face for a moment longer, her eyes pleading.

He turned slightly away and bent down to the child. "How's the kite, pal?"

"It doesn't fly nearly as well without you."

The hint was so transparent that Lindsay felt embarrassed for Beep. His desires couldn't have been any plainer if he'd got down on his knees and begged.

"I'm afraid that's your imagination, Benjamin," Gibb said easily. "Don't forget I'm the one who underestimated the air currents around the courthouse and almost wrapped the kite around the clock tower."

"Wouldn't that have impressed the fire department, getting a call to rescue a kite?" Lindsay murmured.

Beep grinned. "Hey, that'd be fun!"

"I'm sorry I mentioned it. The tour's moving on, Beep—we'd better catch up." She put a hand on his shoulder to urge him forward.

Beep resisted. "Are you coming, too, Gibb?"

Gibb shook his head. "Sorry. I've got work to do."

"Oh. Well, maybe I'll see you this weekend then."

Lindsay couldn't bear the hopeful note in his voice, and she intervened. "I doubt it, Beep. Gibb has *lots* of work, I understand."

Gibb caught her arm as she started to walk away. "Run along, Benjamin," he said gruffly. "I'll talk to you later."

Beep looked from his mother to Gibb and scurried off after the tour group.

"I'm responsible for those children," Lindsay said. "If you'll stop manhandling me and let me catch up—"

Gibb let go of her arm. "This will only take a moment. I don't need you to manage me, Lindsay, or to interpret for me."

"I don't want Beep to be hurt. You said yourself you don't have time for him."

"And I'm perfectly capable of making that clear to Benjamin, without your help. What are you so afraid of, Lindsay? Do you really think I'm cruel enough to raise a child's hopes and then squash them on purpose?" Gibb's voice was soft, relentless. "Or are you afraid I *won't* let him down?"

She met his gaze then, defiantly. "Of course you'd let him down, Gibb—sooner or later. You're incapable of doing anything else." She turned on her heel and hurried away, but she knew that he stood there and watched till the little band was out of sight.

The tour ended an hour later in the company lunchroom with Ben handing out a tiny, noisy, battery-powered toy to each child as a souvenir of the visit.

Kathy Russell murmured, "Boy, am I glad these kids will be going straight home after the tour, so I won't have to contend with twenty-two noisemakers for the rest of the day."

Lindsay smiled. "I'll suggest to Daddy that he might want to switch to something quieter—flashlights, maybe. But I don't think he'll do it. He's almost as fond of those silly toys as the kids are."

Dave Jonas had come in for his afternoon break just in time to hear the exchange, and he snorted as he dropped a couple of coins into a nearby vending machine. "Just don't ask the efficiency expert about it, or he'll eliminate the giveaways altogether." He stuck his candy bar into his shirt pocket and poured a cup of coffee from an enormous urn nearby. "In fact, there's talk he's either going to start charging us for coffee or make us bring our own."

"I'm not surprised there's talk," Lindsay said. "There always is. But you don't really think Gibb would do anything so petty, do you, Dave?"

"Don't tell me you're standing up for the ex, Lindsay."

"I'm not. But Gibb's not stupid—that kind of action makes no sense. It might save a few pennies, but it would cost thousands of dollars' worth of employee goodwill."

"Why should he care? He won't be here for long. But you may be right that the coffee's too small an item to bother with. The last I heard he was spending his time going over the employees' contract with a fine-tooth comb."

And heaven knew, Lindsay thought, Gibb could save more by eliminating a few benefits than by taking out the coffee machine. Though, she reminded herself, the fact that he was reading the contract didn't mean he was searching for loopholes. It was a sensible part of a complete survey of the business.

Still, she wondered if Ben knew about it.

Dave settled at a nearby table and ripped open his candy bar, adding thoughtfully, "Maybe somebody should warn Gardner that messing around with things like employee perks could be hazardous to his health."

Lindsay's throat tightened. "Is that a threat?"

Dave shrugged. "I suppose it could be taken that way." He bit into the candy and added, "Hey, don't look at me like that, Lindsay. I'm not the one who said it first."

That was all he would tell her, however, and by the time Lindsay helped usher the chattering children onto the school bus and returned to the lunchroom, Dave's break was over and he'd gone back to his work station.

It was only talk, anyway, she told herself. Everything was uncertain right now, so of course the employees were concerned, even upset. When their livelihoods were involved, people often said things they didn't mean. Dave himself would never consider violence as a means of negotiation, and probably it had been only an idle threat anyway, spoken in frustration and fear rather than with serious intent.

Thoughtfully, she wandered up to the main offices. As long as she was in the building, she might as well pick up the Armentrout Trust's mail. Though her father had said he'd bring it to her, he'd obviously forgotten in the press of business.

Ben's secretary was away from her desk, but Lindsay knew where Louise kept the trust's file. There wasn't much mail—just a couple of letters asking for contributions, a bank statement and some routine legal forms that needed Lindsay's signature.

She reached into the top desk drawer for a pen, and the door of Ben's office opened behind her. "Louise, would you bring me—" Gibb said, and stopped suddenly. "Hello, Lindsay. I hope you're finding what you need."

"I'm not snooping, you know," Lindsay said acidly. "I was looking for a pen so I can sign these forms for the trust."

"Try the holder on the corner of the desk." He pointed to a big ceramic mug bristling with pens and pencils. "I imagine at least one of those has ink in it."

Lindsay bit her lip. She hated looking like a fool—and Gibb had a positive gift for making her play the role. He obviously didn't intend to go away, either, for he sat down on the edge of Louise's desk and folded his arms, watching her.

She was uncomfortable under the scrutiny, and her hand quivered. Her signature came out looking very strange, but there was no way to patch it up, so she folded the document and slipped it into the return envelope. "Is Daddy here?" she asked.

"He hasn't come back from the tour yet."

"It's over—he must have gotten sidetracked somewhere. I'll leave him a note then, if you'll allow me to get a scratch pad out of Louise's drawer."

Gibb settled more comfortably onto the desk. "Sure. Unless I can help?"

"Not with this. I need to know how much funding I can expect for the trust next month, so I can start deciding what we'll do with it." She found a stenographer's notebook and tore out a blank page. He was looking at her rather oddly, she thought, and remembered the discussion they'd had about whether she was to be trusted not to dip into the funds for her own purposes. "Or," she added, "since it's not entirely up to me, perhaps it's more accurate to say I'll decide what action I'll propose to the board of directors."

Gibb didn't argue the point. "Surely you plan farther ahead than next month."

"Not a lot. The money's intended to do good. If it's sitting in a savings account, nobody benefits except the bank."

"Do you mean to tell me you don't have the money on hand to answer the begging letters you've been getting?"

"We're different than most foundations—we don't have to depend on random contributions, since we get a payment each month from the plant. I just need to know precisely what it'll be." Lindsay's voice trailed off, and she looked at him warily from the corner of her eye. There was something about his tone... "Don't tell me you're reading the trust's mail, too," she challenged. "I saw it had all been opened, but I didn't think you'd descend to snooping."

He didn't bother to deny it. "I need to know what's going on in all aspects of this business."

"The trust is separate from the plant!"

"Technically, maybe—but as long as it's getting part of the profits, it's my concern. Perhaps you'd better come into my office where we can discuss this privately." He slid off the desk and started toward the door he'd emerged from.

"*Your* office?" Lindsay said dryly. "It still has Daddy's name on the door."

She'd expected that he'd be embarrassed by his slip of the tongue, but Gibb only shrugged. "All the important paperwork is in there. Ben thought it would be easier to move him rather than all the files I needed."

The logic was perfectly reasonable, but that fact didn't soothe Lindsay. No wonder the workers on the factory floor were uneasy, she thought. It must look to them as if Ben Armentrout had abdicated all responsibility.

Gibb held the door for her and indicated one of Ben's deep leather armchairs. But Lindsay didn't sit down. "Is this how Triangle always works?" she asked acidly. "By taking over a place lock, stock and barrel?"

"Absolutely. How could we possibly rejuvenate a foundering business without full authority to act wherever it turns out to be necessary?"

"This plant isn't foundering. It has its difficulties, but it's hardly on the brink of disaster."

"I beg to differ with you. If it wasn't for the division that produces small batteries for consumers—the kind of thing your father loves to give away to school kids— the whole company might well have gone down the river by now. Or hadn't you realized how much of Ben's sales were to defense contractors who are out of business now that the Cold War's over?"

Lindsay shook her head. "I hadn't thought about it."

"You only think about how to spend the profits—I suppose I should have realized that."

She raised her chin at the tart note in his voice. "Now see here, Gibb—"

"That's what I called you in to talk about," he went on, as if he hadn't heard the interruption. "The question of profits. At the moment, you see, there aren't any, so there won't be any percentage for the Armentrout Trust this month. And if you take my advice, you won't count on a contribution for some time to come."

CHAPTER SIX

LINDSAY'S knees started to shake, and she sank into the leather armchair. "You're doing this to get even with me, aren't you, Gibb?"

He shook his head. "No, Lindsay. I'll show you the books if you like. There is no profit—in fact, the plant will just barely break even this month. Even that's something of a miracle, considering that one of the production lines hasn't paid its own way in a year."

"But that's ridiculous! The profits have been smaller lately, yes—that's why Daddy wanted advice from Triangle—but nothing like the situation you're talking about. And in any case, you can't just shut off the trust."

"Why can't I? Because it'll be inconvenient for you if I do? Dammit, Lindsay, when are you going to get it through your head that every decision I make does not revolve around you? This is purely a matter of economics."

She shook her head. "That's not what I mean at all. If word gets out that there's no money for the trust—whether it's true or not—there'll be panic. Everybody in Elmwood knows how the trust is funded. You might as well shout the news that the plant is going broke from the courthouse steeple." She took a deep breath. "In fact, you'd be better off if you did announce it, because you might sidetrack a few of the rumors that way."

Gibb's eyes had narrowed, but his voice was level. "It wasn't exactly a brilliant idea to set the trust up on a percentage basis, was it? I suppose everybody in town

94

knows what the percentage is, too, and can figure out the net profits—when there are any—to the last penny?''

''Of course not.''

''I wouldn't bet against it. It's a little late to avoid that problem now, but at least it explains what your father did last month.''

Lindsay frowned. ''What do you mean? I told you, last month the plant made a profit—not enormous, but reasonable—and the foundation got a nice chunk of it. Now, just thirty days later, you expect me to believe there's nothing? What's gone wrong so suddenly?'' She looked at him suspiciously. ''The only change I can see is *you*, Gibb.''

''So you think I must be cooking the books to make the picture look worse than it actually is? Why would I bother?''

She didn't answer.

''Last month there wasn't any profit, either, but your father very quietly underwrote the plant's regular contribution to the trust. The money came out of his personal draw, and he did his best to conceal where he'd shifted it from one account to the other.''

Lindsay bristled. ''Are you saying he did something wrong?''

''No. What he did wasn't illegal or even unethical. It's his own business and his own money, and he can do what he wants as long as he's not trying to defraud anyone.''

''Which he obviously wasn't,'' Lindsay said stiffly.

''I didn't say he was. But it was hardly wise not to tell you what he was doing. Personally, I'd bet he wasn't as concerned about the town's reaction as about yours— he couldn't bear to tell you about the shortfall, so he made up the difference himself and hoped that by this month things would get better, so you wouldn't have to know."

"And here you are, gleefully telling me that you've made it worse instead!"

"I'm not exactly gleeful about it—and I didn't cause the shortfall, either. I just think it's time Ben stopped bending over backward to protect his little girl from the harsher facts of life—even if you're disillusioned about him because of it."

Lindsay glared at him. As if he knew anything about it! Yes, Ben had had a tendency to wrap her in cotton once—but that had been a long time ago. How dare Gibb judge her now on the basis of things that had happened so far in the past?

"Perhaps we shouldn't forget that you've got a built-in reason to want the plant to look awful," Lindsay said bitterly.

Gibb frowned. "I do?"

"Oh, yes. The worse the business appears, the more of a hero you'll be to your bosses at Triangle when you rescue it from looming disaster."

"There is that, of course." Gibb's voice was level. "Always assuming that I manage to save it at all."

Lindsay gasped. "You can't mean you'd just shut it down!"

"Not exactly."

She relaxed. She ought to have realized he'd made the threat only for its shock value—but without thinking, she'd reacted exactly the way he'd no doubt hoped she would.

"We'd sell off the profitable production lines first," Gibb went on, "and then junk whatever was left."

"Daddy would never allow—"

"Ben doesn't have that authority any more. I do."

She stared at him in disbelief.

"Or didn't he tell you those are the terms when Triangle takes on a business challenge? We prefer to save the business, of course, because we make more money that way. But it's not always possible."

She jumped up from her chair. "Now I begin to see. I suppose you've already made up your mind this is going to be one of the failures?"

"Not at all. It depends, you see."

"On what?" Lindsay swallowed a lump in her throat. The suspicion that nagged at her was too incredible to believe, but before she could consider the repercussions, she'd voiced it anyway. "Are you blackmailing me, Gibb?"

He smiled without humor. "Oh, hardly," he said dryly. "I can't think of anything you have that I'd want. Unless, of course..." He slid off the corner of the desk, and suddenly he was looming over her.

Lindsay felt like a hunted rabbit, exposed in the center of a barren field with an eagle circling above, patiently waiting to pounce. She gulped and began, "If I was to call your boss at Triangle and tell him you're exercising personal grudges here..."

"Don't be ridiculous. There's nothing personal about it." Gibb sounded incredibly bored. "If there was, I'd probably be doing things like this."

Lindsay didn't see him move, but even if she had, it would have done her no good; like the rabbit, she was too paralyzed to try to save herself. Gibb's arm felt like a steel trap around her shoulders, and his mouth came down on hers in an abrupt, ferocious, demanding kiss that scorched her lips. His other hand cupped the back of her head, holding her relentlessly close while he plundered her mouth.

She could not pull free, and though she tried to pound her fists against his back, Gibb didn't seem to notice the feeble impact, which was all she could manage.

The kiss must have lasted barely a minute, but it seemed an age to Lindsay, an eternity of time in which memories of very different kisses flooded through her brain. Very different—and yet disturbingly similar, as well. She hadn't realized before that she still remembered the taste of him.

He released her, and Lindsay stumbled back a step, holding her knuckles against her mouth in an instinctive effort to hide the way her lips were quivering. But she was shaking in anger, she told herself, and there was no need to hide that! She flailed out with a open hand, but Gibb caught her arm before she could strike and put her firmly back in her chair.

"Now aren't you glad there's nothing personal involved?" His voice was hoarse.

She was almost too breathless to speak. "If you ever do that again—"

"It was only a demonstration, Lindsay." He looked straight at her, his eyes incredibly dark, and added coolly, "An illustration of how incredibly stupid I'd have to be to base my business decisions on *that*."

The last word, she thought, was loaded with distaste. Lindsay swallowed hard and painfully. It had been a long time since she'd lost her last illusions over how Gibb felt about her. But once upon a time they had meant everything to each other—and it hurt to hear loathing in his voice.

Gibb reached for a business card from the holder on the corner of Ben's desk. Taking a fountain pen from his pocket, he wrote something on the back of it. "Here's Triangle's phone number. I'd suggest you talk to—"

Lindsay shook her head. "Oh, no. You've made your point. If I called, you'd only hold it against Daddy."

"I don't transfer grudges, Lindsay." The harsh note was gone from his voice; he sounded as if he was merely reporting a fact. "I'd only hold it against you—though considering the way we already feel about each other, I doubt it would make any real difference at all."

Lindsay went back to work for the rest of the afternoon, but she didn't accomplish much. She was still burning inside with the fury that he'd roused.

Fury—and pain, as well. It was not physical suffering that nagged at her; though Gibb was certainly strong enough to hurt her, he had not. While her lips felt bruised and swollen, her mirror showed no evidence whatsoever of that relentless kiss—and so Lindsay was forced to conclude that what she felt was more psychic soreness than physical distress.

A carefully built dam inside her seemed to have crumbled under the fierce assault of his kiss, and all the memories Lindsay had buried nine years ago spilled once more into her conscious mind with the raging power of floodwaters.

From every angle, memory assailed her. There were glimpses of the two of them playing tag in the country club swimming pool or cuddling together in one chair before the simulated fire in their little apartment. She could envision the lazy way he used to look at her in the early mornings, when there was still time for loving before he went to work....

This, she told herself firmly, was madness.

It was positively insane to let herself be so affected by a kiss. Especially a kiss that had been given—or perhaps the word was *inflicted*—for all the wrong reasons. There had been passion in it, yes, but it had risen from anger, not sexual attraction. There had been nothing about that kiss that should have reminded her of the early, gentle, loving moments; it should have brought back memories only of the disagreeable times.

It infuriated Lindsay to realize that once more Gibb had proved that he possessed far more self-control than she did. Apart from the slight hoarseness of his voice after he'd kissed her, he'd been perfectly in command of himself. He had always possessed a sort of rigid self-discipline that she had never seen crack, no matter how angry he was. He'd made his point as he'd set out to do, and as far as he was concerned that was the end of it. No doubt by now he was absorbed once more in Ben Armentrout's business problems, and Lindsay was far from his mind.

But Lindsay felt as if an old movie projector had been switched on in her brain. It seemed to be running at the wrong speed, with no sound and the picture flickering madly from scene to scene—but even with her eyes closed she couldn't escape.

She absently wrapped a wedding gift in pink and blue paper patterned with baby rattles and alphabet blocks and apologized profusely when the customer pointed out the error. She agreed with another client that the spring wind outside was awful, and fifteen seconds later commented that the weather was beautiful. When the woman looked at her in astonishment, Lindsay almost panicked, for she only vaguely remembered what she'd said.

After the customer left and the store was quiet once more, she sagged against the cash register counter and swore. It wasn't fair that she should be feeling confused; what she ought to be feeling was offended. Gibb had no right to behave that way. She should have slapped him.

But there was no putting the genie back in the bottle, and for the rest of the afternoon Lindsay suffered the aftereffects. Everything seemed to be brighter, louder, more aromatic—and it all brought back memories. The smell of coffee reminded her of the strong brew that Gibb had preferred, a scent that had usually been her first sensation on waking. The warmth of sunshine pouring through the show window brought back the brief honeymoon they had spent on a Caribbean beach. The sound of the church carillon playing Elmwood's regular Friday afternoon concert reminded her of the way those same bells had pealed in joyous abandon to announce their wedding vows. And that led her to remember the whole afternoon she'd been married—the slickness of white satin, the warmth of her father's arm under her hand as he escorted her down the aisle, the scent of roses rising from her bouquet, the look in Gibb's eyes as he waited for her...

There had been an unusual softness in his face, she remembered, and an uneasy pride, and something else that she'd had no time to wonder about then. Something she hadn't even thought about since.

Funny that she recalled it so effortlessly, though. She could picture him as he waited at the altar—a younger Gibb, without a thread of silver in his hair, without the air of confidence he wore so easily now. He had looked...

Bewildered, Lindsay realized. He had stared at her that day as if he couldn't quite make himself believe where he was and what he was doing. Almost as if he was caught in a nightmare—knowing he was asleep, but unable to awaken and act.

It was too bad he hadn't backed out, she thought. Dreadful as the consequences would have seemed at the time, the action would have saved them both a lot of trouble.

Lindsay sighed. "I should have run," she muttered. But she had been so desperately in love.

"Run where?" Ben Armentrout asked.

Lindsay jumped. She had been too lost in the taunting replay of her wedding to hear the bell on Potpourri's door, and Ben was almost beside her when he spoke.

"Oh—just run away, I suppose," she said lamely. "Anywhere but Elmwood."

His eyes were warm. "It would have been mighty lonely around here without you and Beep." He cleared his throat. "I brought the trust's mail over. You left it on Louise's desk this afternoon."

Lindsay had forgotten. She'd still been shaking with anger and frustration—and something else, as well— when she'd walked through the outer office. She probably wouldn't have noticed if the place had been on fire, she thought, so it was no surprise she hadn't remembered the tidy bundle of envelopes she'd left on the corner of the secretary's desk. Not that it made much difference, since there was so little money to fund the requests anyway. "Thanks, Daddy." She tucked the envelopes into a slot beside the cash register. "You're out of the office early."

"I've got a meeting of the hospital board. There's a letter in there from the local shelter for battered women, by the way—it just came in this afternoon's mail. It sounds as if the shelter is having an emergency of its own."

Lindsay didn't bother to look for the letter. "Too bad it didn't happen last month, when the trust had some cash."

Ben was silent for a long moment. "I gather Gibb told you."

Lindsay nodded. "Why didn't you tell me yourself, Daddy?"

"I didn't want to admit it, I suppose. Even though I knew things were bad, I hoped it wouldn't be necessary to cut off the trust."

Something Gibb had said that afternoon had been nagging at her, Lindsay realized. He'd said Ben should stop protecting her, even at the cost of Lindsay's disillusionment. "And last month? Why were you trying so hard to protect me?"

He smiled faintly. "A parent always wants to protect his child, honey."

Lindsay couldn't exactly argue that point, considering how far she'd gone in her efforts to keep Beep safe. "Were you afraid I wouldn't love you any more if you weren't successful?"

"I know better than to think that. But I hate to see you disappointed—in me, or in anything else."

She put her arms around him and held him close.

"I'll write a check, Lindsay, for the shelter and the other things the trust needs this month. How much—"

She was shaking her head. "No. You've done more than enough. I can't take money you'll need yourself, if..." Her voice was trembling, despite her best efforts. "If the plant doesn't make it."

Ben handed her his handkerchief. "I'd like the answer to that question myself," he said soberly.

"Hasn't Gibb even told you what's going on? Given you an idea of what to expect?"

Ben shook his head. "Not yet."

"And you're just supposed to sit quietly by while he decides what to do with your company?"

"That's the way Triangle works, Lindsay. When they agree to take on a business, they're entirely in charge."

She shook her head in disbelief. "And they send in a single consultant with unlimited power—and trust that it won't be abused. How can they do that?"

"For one thing, they don't let just anybody do that work, you know. Don't underestimate Gibb, my dear."

"Do you even know how long he's been with them?"

"From the beginning." Ben sounded a little surprised. "Didn't he tell you? It's still just the three of them, you know, though they've built up quite a support staff."

"The three of them?"

"The three founding partners. Triangle—get it?"

"You're telling me Gibb's a full third of this business?"

Ben nodded. "That's a good way to put it. It's why they're so careful about the jobs they take, you see, because every project requires one of the partners to be on the scene. It limits the amount they can do, so—"

Lindsay was shaking her head. "And I threatened to report him to his boss," she muttered.

"Really?" Ben was obviously amused. "What did Gibb say?"

"He gave me the phone number. Daddy, how could you do this? Put yourself in Gibb's hands like this?"

Ben stopped smiling. "I'm getting old, Lindsay," he said finally. "And my business is in trouble. If there is to be any sort of legacy for you and Beep, I need help."

Tears stung her eyes. "I just hope you didn't put it to Gibb that way."

"No," Ben said. "But then, he didn't ask."

He left a few minutes later, already late for his meeting. Lindsay repaired her mascara and started dusting display shelves. Her nerves were too frazzled to allow her to settle to anything else, and the memories continued to flash despite all her efforts. Trying to fend them off, she concluded finally, was like fighting a migraine—exhausting and ultimately useless.

Gibb almost didn't see the bicycle; it was lying flat on the gravel at the verge of the highway, and he was past it before he saw the heap of what looked like rags lying beside it. Another full second passed before the reality registered, but his reflexes had already reacted. Even before his conscious mind recognized that he'd seen not a pile of cloth but a small body, he'd slammed on the Lincoln's brakes and the car had shuddered to a halt in the middle of the traffic lane.

Gibb didn't even bother to check for oncoming traffic; he left the car door open, crossed the highway in half a dozen strides and stopped beside the bicycle with his heart in his mouth. The little body was huddled in a heap, half under the metal frame—and lying far too still for first aid to do much good. He should have called for help on the car phone. Precious seconds were ticking by.

Beep unrolled himself and slid out from under the bicycle frame. "Hi!"

Gibb looked at the child in disbelief. Beep's face was grimy with road dust; there was a streak of what looked like oil on his nose, and his hair was standing up at all angles. But he was obviously unhurt—and happy to see Gibb.

"What in the *hell*—" Gibb said, and had to stop because of the tremor in his voice. "I thought you'd been hit by a car!"

"Oh, no. I was very careful to stay off the highway. But I'm not used to riding on gravel and my bike threw the chain. At least I thought it was just thrown, so I was trying to get it back on, but I guess it snapped instead." He held up the broken end.

"What were you doing out here in the first place? You're a good mile from home!"

"I was coming to the plant to see you. We didn't have a chance to talk today with Mom around, so—"

"Have you never heard of telephones?" Gibb's voice was almost ferocious.

The child's chin wobbled. "It was our secret," he said, in little more than a whisper.

"Oh, for—" Gibb swallowed the rest of the oath. "Here, let's pick up the bike and get you back to town."

"Thank you, sir."

"Don't thank me till you know what I'm going to do."

Beep's eyes widened.

"As a matter of fact, I think you deserve to be spanked. But since that's not my business, I'm going to take you home to your mother instead."

"That's worse," Beep muttered.

The bicycle was unwieldy; as Gibb lifted it into the trunk, the front wheel turned and rubbed against the car's shining paint. Beep gasped.

"It's only dust. It'll wipe off," Gibb said, and caught the child's arm as he started to move toward the car. "But not with your sleeve, all right?"

"I was just trying—"

"You're exceptionally trying, Benjamin. Get in."

Beep's eyes roved over the car's luxurious interior. "Why do you always call me Benjamin?"

"Isn't it your name?"

"Yeah. But nobody but my mother calls me that, and then only when I'm in big trouble."

"I think I'd brace myself if I were you," Gibb advised.

"You wouldn't have to tell her," Beep wheedled. "I was only coming to see you, and since I found you after all I won't do it again."

"Good try."

Beep sighed. "I only wanted to ask if you'd thought of a job for me."

"Nope. I'm having nothing further to do with this. Once I've delivered you to your mother, I'm done."

"She'll ground me. And then I can't get any kind of job, and I won't be able to buy her a birthday present."

"Sorry. But you should have thought of that before you pulled this stunt." The car slowed as he turned toward the business district, and he looked down at the golden-blond head in the seat beside him. Something like sympathy tugged at his heart. But he didn't want to think about that, so he asked, "Don't you get tired of being called Beep?"

The child shrugged. "I'm used to it."

There seemed to be nothing else to say.

Potpourri's lights were off when the car pulled up in front, and Gibb glanced at his watch. "It's after five," he pointed out. "And the shop's closed. Any idea where your mother will be?"

Beep's face paled, making the freckles stand out. "Upstairs in the apartment, probably. The entrance is in the back. But you don't have to take me around." He met Gibb's eyes with an effort at innocence. "If it's too much trouble..."

"You just never give up, do you?" Gibb said curiously.

He parked the Lincoln next to a little paved courtyard behind the building and looked around it with interest. Lindsay must use it as a patio when the weather was nice; there was a wrought-iron table and several matching chairs. In a corner was what looked like a small fountain, still covered to protect it from the winter cold. Tucked as it was into the angle of the buildings, the courtyard was a quiet, well-protected, private little spot.

The back door had a combination lock. "I lost my key last year," Beep said as he twisted the dial, "so Mom had this put in instead."

"I won't look," Gibb promised solemnly.

He could hear the soft murmur of her voice as they climbed the stairs, but he couldn't make out the words. Beep was dawdling, taking each step as if it was Mount Everest, but Gibb didn't mind—it gave him a moment to brace himself.

The staircase opened into a little hallway right off the kitchen area, and because of his height he could see Lindsay well before he reached the top of the stairs. She had her back to him, and the telephone to her ear, and he wasted a moment in pure appreciation of the view. She had the sort of elegant slenderness that didn't rob her of feminine curves, and the sweater and slacks she wore made the most of her figure. He still had no trouble picturing her wearing nothing at all.

Just being around her had been difficult enough in his apartment last weekend, but in the close confines of Ben Armentrout's little office this afternoon, her presence had been overwhelming. And the results should have been predictable. Kissing her had been a major mistake, of course—it had only fed the flame of imagination.

Lindsay said, "Well, thanks anyway, Betty. If you see him . . . yes, please. Goodbye." She clicked a button on the phone and started to dial again.

Gibb put a hand on the child's shoulder and urged him forward. Beep said, almost cheerfully, "Hi, Mom! Did you miss me?"

Lindsay dropped the phone and spun around. "Benjamin, where have you—"

Gibb watched her eyes narrow and darken as she spotted him, and he knew that kissing her hadn't just been a mistake, but a damned stupid stunt.

"Well." Her voice was flat. "I suppose I should have expected you'd be involved."

"I don't see why," Gibb said mildly.

"Really? After all that talk about holding grudges, I'm supposed to be surprised that you'd take this way—" She stopped abruptly and looked at Beep. "What happened to you?"

"My bike chain broke, so Gibb brought me home. That's all."

"That's why you're late? A broken chain?"

Beep nodded solemnly.

Lindsay looked at him for a long moment, and then raised her eyes to Gibb's face. "I suppose I owe you an apology. Thanks for bringing him home."

"Don't you want to know where I found him?"

"Oh, Gibb—" Disgust dripped from Beep's voice.

"Sorry, pal, but it was a dangerous thing to do, and I'm not going to help cover it up." He leaned indolently against the refrigerator door and looked at Lindsay. "I came across him about a mile outside town, on the highway."

"On the *highway*? Beep, where were you going?"

Beep bit his lip.

"I haven't a clue," Gibb said easily. "If the chain hadn't broken, it's hard to tell how far he'd have gotten."

His hand still rested on the child's shoulder, and he felt a little of the tension seep away as Beep realized the rest of his secret wouldn't be shared. A moment later, it was back, though, as Lindsay stooped over her son.

"Benjamin Patrick Gardner, you are grounded to this apartment, except for school, till further notice."

She sounded like a judge pronouncing sentence, Gibb thought.

"Geez, Mom," Beep protested, "that's not fair. At least tell me how long!"

"All right. Make it till you're twenty-one. Or dead—which at this rate won't be any time at all. You know better than to take your bike on the highway!"

"Well, you won't have to worry about that any more. If I have to stay locked in here till I'm grown up—"

Gibb moved a little. "Don't be impudent to your mother."

Beep grumbled, but he shut up.

"Thank you," Lindsay said.

Gibb thought she sounded surprised. "Don't mention it. But as long as we're on the subject, don't you think you're being a bit too harsh? I didn't bring him home in order to get him punished for life, you know."

"It's not your concern, Gibb."

"Would you rather I'd have just left him there?"

She sighed. "Of course not." She turned to Beep. "Okay, you're right about setting a limit to the punishment. You're grounded for three weeks, and after that I'm impounding your bike for another three."

"Mom!" Beep howled. He made the name sound as if it had three syllables.

"Personally," Gibb murmured, "I think that's still harsh."

"Who asked you?" Lindsay snapped.

He didn't pause. "Because the punishment affects me, too. You see, Lindsay, Beep has already agreed to work for me tomorrow, and if he doesn't keep his word I'll be in a bind."

Lindsay was livid. *"What?"*

Beep's face was practically glowing.

Gibb looked at him, and his hand tightened on the child's shoulder. "Yes," he said steadily. "He's promised to wash my car."

CHAPTER SEVEN

LINDSAY'S eight years of motherhood hadn't been in vain; she knew perfectly well when a story carried the aroma of week-old codfish. She had to admit, though, that it wasn't Gibb's fault she knew he was fudging the truth. The man could have made a fortune at a poker table. But she'd never had any trouble seeing through Beep.

Not that it was any challenge right now, she thought dryly. Her son's face was almost luminous with surprise.

Well, it was possible the punishment she'd assigned had been a little too harsh—though she wasn't about to admit that to Gibb. In the meantime, while she was thinking the matter over, it wouldn't do Beep any harm to have a job to occupy a little of his energy. Grounding him wouldn't do much good if all he did with his time was catch up on his comic-book reading.

And, Lindsay thought with a tinge of wry humor, it might be interesting to see if Gibb squirmed when she agreed. She couldn't quite imagine him turning that brand-new Lincoln over to an eight-year-old—but it would be something worth watching if he did.

"I certainly wouldn't want to put you to any inconvenience, Gibb," she said sweetly. "And we all know how important that car is to you, so I know keeping it clean is a priority. I'm going to allow Beep to fulfill his promise—"

"I can?" Beep gave a whoop. "Thanks, Mom!"

Lindsay went on firmly, "But I meant what I said about him leaving the building, so you'll have to bring the car here, Gibb. He can wash it in the courtyard out back, where I can keep an eye on him."

Beep seemed a little doubtful about that, but after one quick look at his mother he was wise enough not to argue.

To Lindsay's disappointment, Gibb didn't even flinch. "That's fine. Meet me behind the building at one o'clock, Benjamin."

"Sure. You called me Beep a little while ago, you know."

"Did I? I must be slipping in my old age. I'll see you tomorrow, then. Will the back door lock behind me, Lindsay?"

Lindsay nodded and stood in the middle of her kitchen, listening, till the sound of his footsteps on the stairs had faded away. Then she looked thoughtfully at her son. Beep was on his knees on the kitchen floor with a bit of nylon cord, teasing the cat. Spats leaped at the frayed end and missed, and Beep giggled.

"You're in a surprisingly good mood for someone who's just lost three weeks of freedom," Lindsay observed.

Beep didn't even look up. "I don't mind being grounded, as long as I can still see Gibb."

The innocent comment annoyed Lindsay beyond all reason, and she said sharply, "In that case, we may have to find a punishment that's more effective. Now stop tormenting Spats and wash up and set the table for dinner."

Beep gave her a puzzled look. But he didn't dawdle, just rolled up the cord, stuck it in his pocket and went off toward the bathroom, whistling.

Lindsay sighed. She knew when she was beaten; the pair of them had gotten around her with no trouble at all. She'd just make sure to learn from the experience, so that next time . . .

Of course, by the next time Beep got himself into major trouble, Gibb would probably be long gone.

She wondered why that didn't make her feel relieved.

Saturday afternoons were usually busy at Potpourri, so Lindsay always scheduled one of her employees to help out. The extra pair of hands left her with more freedom to keep an eye on Beep, and sometimes, in the rare dull hours, to catch up on some of the behind-the-scenes work. But on that particular Saturday she found herself almost wishing that her employee had called in sick and left her to handle the entire shop by herself. It would have given her less time to think, and less time to watch what was going on out in her courtyard.

She supposed she should have expected that Gibb wouldn't simply deliver his car into Beep's inexpert hands. Instead, he'd stayed to show the child how to do the job, and every time she'd looked out, the two of them had been side by side, Beep watching Gibb and then carefully imitating his actions.

At midafternoon, when the black paint was finally gleaming and dry and polished, Lindsay was relieved. But the next time she peeked out, thinking it was past time to end Beep's reprieve from punishment, the car doors stood open and the scent of leather polish filled the air.

"Are you going to be done soon?" she asked politely.

Beep poked his head out from the floor of the backseat, a smear of polish on his chin, and grinned.

"Hi, Mom! I never knew there was so much work to washing a car!"

"He's pretty good at it, too," Gibb added. "Short people have an advantage sometimes. He can crawl into places I can't."

"I'm delighted to hear it," Lindsay said and went back to her customers. She didn't look outside for another hour after that, and when she did, Beep was lying on the pavement, his legs under the front of the car, polishing the chrome trim on the bumper. That time she didn't even bother to ask how long the job might take.

When she went back to the shop again, one of her neighbors from across the square was waiting for her at the cash register with a crystal bell and a credit card. While Lindsay rang up the sale, Mrs. Johnson said, "I got to thinking after you gave me Mr. Gardner's dues the other day that perhaps the Courthouse Squares should have a little party to welcome him. I mean, since he's new to the community as well as the neighborhood—"

Lindsay wanted to groan.

"I'll be happy to host it," the woman went on. "I thought next Sunday would be best, in the late afternoon—just tea and things, nothing fancy. He could get to meet his new neighbors, at least."

"Oh, why not have a full-fledged housewarming while we're at it?" Lindsay said, almost under her breath.

Mrs. Johnson looked at her blankly for a moment, then smiled broadly. "What a delightful idea! Not that he really needs anything, living at the Olivers'. But it would be cute to have some fun little gifts."

Lindsay bit her lip. In the face of that enthusiasm, she could hardly admit that she'd intended the suggestion to be purely sarcastic. That was what happened when she let her tongue run away with her! "Maybe you'd better ask Gibb first. He may not think much of the idea."

"Oh, I have," Mrs. Johnson said. "I came up from the park and saw him washing the car out back with your little boy. What a nice man he is, to do that."

Two aisles away, Lindsay caught a glimpse of Skye Oliver's dark head, bent to one side as if she was listening intently. Lindsay hadn't seen her come into the store; Skye must have arrived while Lindsay was in the courtyard.

"Isn't he, though," Lindsay said, keeping her voice carefully level. "Would you like me to gift-wrap the bell?"

"Oh, no, it's just for my collection."

Skye came up to the counter. "Lindsay, does this picture frame really cost forty dollars?"

Her tone, Lindsay thought, implied that nothing in the store was worth that much. "If that's what the tag says, yes."

"Oh." Skye put the frame down beside the cash register and smiled at the other customer. "I couldn't help overhearing your plans, Mrs. Johnson. I'd love to help with your party for Gibb—it sounds like tremendous fun."

"I'd really intended to invite only the Courthouse Squares, Skye."

"Of course I wouldn't dream of inviting myself!" Skye sounded shocked at the notion. "Though as far as that's concerned, I've always considered that I'm sort of an honorary member, since I look after my parents' place so much."

And especially right now, Lindsay thought cynically, when she was taking such good care of the Olivers' apartment.

"I'd just stay in the background, of course. You know, pour tea and that sort of thing. And of course if you need any help planning or shopping—" She stopped for a breath, and added simply, "You see, Gibb and I have become . . . very close."

Mrs. Johnson rolled her eyes in Lindsay's direction and said, with an edge to her voice, "I see. Well, that would be lovely, Skye. I'll call you and let you know what you can do to help." She picked up her package and hurried out.

Accepting the inevitable and making a fast getaway, Lindsay deduced, before Skye could decide that a Saturday-night dance party would be better for everyone, and far more to Gibb's taste than Sunday tea.

Skye leaned on the counter. "What's this about Gibb baby-sitting your kid, Lindsay?"

"Pardon me? I didn't realize anyone had said anything about baby-sitting. Do you want to buy that frame?"

"Not for forty bucks, I don't. So they're washing the car together. What a nice little domestic picture that must make! It was your idea, I suppose?"

"It not only wasn't my idea, Skye, it isn't even my car they're washing."

Skye's jaw dropped. "You mean he's letting a little kid—"

"Yes." Lindsay smiled sweetly. "It does make one think, doesn't it?" She picked up the frame and carried it across the store to put it in its place, and while she was occupied, Skye hurried out.

She'd hit the nail on the head with that careless comment, though, Lindsay realized. The whole situation *did* make her think—far too much.

Toward the end of the day, business dropped off, and Lindsay left her assistant to close the shop while she went up to the apartment to start dinner. But though she got the chicken out of the refrigerator right away, she didn't begin to cook it. Instead she found herself standing by the big window at the back of the apartment, the package of meat still in her hand, looking down on the scene below.

Gibb was polishing the sliding glass panel in the car's roof—no doubt because Beep couldn't reach it. He'd taken his jacket off, and the warm sunshine fell softly across the back of the close-fitting knit shirt he wore. Lindsay noted the rhythmic movement of his arm and the way the muscles rippled in his back, and remembered watching him from their little apartment above the carriage house as he'd polished a different car—the old and slightly rusty Chevy, which was one of the few assets he'd brought to their marriage—with the same attention, care and pride he was lavishing on the Lincoln.

Beep gave a last swipe to the chrome trim on the driver's door and fanned himself with his polishing cloth. Gibb turned and looked at him, smiling. Lindsay couldn't hear what he said, but her imagination had no trouble supplying a dozen possibilities. None of which, she reminded herself, was probably anywhere close to the truth.

A nice little domestic picture, Skye had called it, with an ironic twist in her voice. But there was no irony in Lindsay as she stood and watched, just a soul-deep longing that the snapshot she saw could have been more than just a disjointed moment out of time. She was wishing that this could have been the reality, wishing that they had been a family, the three of them together....

No, she thought. *I can't still care about Gibb. Not after what he did to me.*

Beep had begun gathering up the tools and polishing cloths. With a start, Lindsay realized she was still standing by the window with the package of raw chicken in her hand, and hastily she turned to the kitchen.

Chunks of chicken were sizzling in the wok, and she was chopping an onion, when Beep came up the stairs with a bundle. Lindsay took one look at it and said, "What are you doing with my best velour towels?"

Beep looked from her face to the bundle as if he'd like to deny that he was holding anything at all. "They polished real good," he offered uncertainly.

"I'll bet."

"Grandpa used them when he fixed the faucet."

"Well, he didn't have permission, either. Put the towels in the laundry room—I'll see if I can save them. And then wash up for supper. Grandpa's coming to eat with us tonight because he's got other plans for lunch tomorrow."

"Does that mean a really nice dinner?"

"We're having a chicken stir-fry with rice. Why?"

"Can I invite Gibb?"

"I seem to recall we agreed that when you're grounded you can't invite guests over, either." She added the onion to the wok. "Get going, Beep."

He moved off toward the tiny laundry room, and she realized for the first time that Gibb was standing at the top of the stairs. He must have heard that last exchange, she thought, and to her annoyance she felt guilty color washing over her face. That was silly, she told herself. She had nothing to feel guilty about.

"I'm sorry about the towels," Gibb said. "I didn't realize where he was getting them. I'll replace them, if you like."

She didn't look at him. "Oh, it doesn't matter. I suppose they'll wash."

"Well, let me know. I'll see you later, then."

"Gibb—" Her throat felt tight, and the words came out all wrong. "You can stay for dinner if you want."

He didn't answer, just looked at her as if he was studying her for a test.

"I mean," Lindsay went on, still a bit awkwardly, "it was very kind of you to spend the afternoon with Beep, and I'd like you to have dinner with us."

There was a long silence before he said quietly, "I'd like to stay."

It was stupid, Lindsay told herself, to feel relief—except, of course, that she'd made such a hash of the invitation she wouldn't have been surprised if he'd been too insulted to accept, and she was glad he'd understood what she meant.

She turned quickly to the refrigerator to get a green pepper and a stalk of celery, and said, "I've got beer and wine, if you'd like some."

"The beer, please. It wasn't hot today, but that was thirsty work."

Lindsay opened the bottle and set a glass on the breakfast bar that overlooked the stove. Gibb perched on the edge of a stool and watched as she chopped up the celery and pepper.

He took a long swallow of his beer and asked, "Does Benjamin's father ever see him?"

Lindsay's knife slipped. She didn't look up. "No. He doesn't live here."

"That's too bad. He really wants a man in his life. Not that it's any of my business."

"That's true." She pushed the celery into the wok and began to clean a couple of carrots. "I hear you're going to be the star of a party next weekend. Lucky you—the Courthouse Squares don't honor every new member that way."

Gibb grimaced. "Mrs. Johnson sort of insisted."

"Well, I'm sure you'll enjoy it," Lindsay said dryly. She was thinking of Skye. It was hard to tell what plans that young woman would come up with, given a whole week to think it over.

She chopped the carrot and added it to the wok, and Gibb finished his beer and shook his head when she offered a second one. It was an almost companionable silence, she thought, except that Gibb seemed to be intently watching every motion she made.

"I wonder what happened to Beep," she said finally.

"Want me to go check?"

"Not just now." She debated for an instant and made up her mind. He needed to know about those threats; she'd have told him yesterday if she hadn't gotten sidetracked with the trust. "Gibb, has there been any trouble at the plant?"

"Depends on what you mean by trouble. If the fact that it's leaking cash isn't enough—"

Lindsay shook her head. "No. I mean employee trouble. It's just something I heard, and maybe it's only idle talk and not a threat at all, but—"

He drew circles on the breakfast bar with the bottom of his empty glass. "What is it, Lindsay?"

She took a deep breath. "Somebody told me that perhaps you should be warned that messing around with the employees' perks could be hazardous to your health."

"Jonas, I suppose."

Reluctantly, Lindsay said, "He's the one who told me, yes. He also said it wasn't his idea—and I believe him."

Ben Armentrout's voice boomed from the top of the stairs. "It certainly smells good in here!"

"I wouldn't worry about it, Lindsay," Gibb said quietly, and stood up to greet Ben.

Just then Beep returned and stood wide-eyed in the center of the living room, staring at Gibb, before he let out a shout and came running. "Gibb! Are you staying after all? Come and see my room. I want to show you—"

Lindsay raised her voice. "I believe there's a small matter of table setting that needs to come first, Beep."

"Oh, Mom . . ."

Gibb set his empty glass and bottle beside the sink and said, "Show me where things are, Benjamin, and I'll help."

Ben helped himself to a glass of wine from the refrigerator and sat down at the breakfast bar to watch. "Well," he said, under his breath. The single syllable held a world of meaning.

Lindsay glanced at the pair setting the table and said, "It's only dinner. Don't get any ideas, Daddy."

"Me? I haven't had an idea in years." Ben pulled a slip of paper from his shirt pocket. "Here's a check for the foundation, to go to the crisis center."

"Daddy, I told you—"

"It's not from me, my dear. I mentioned the problem at the hospital board meeting yesterday, and one of the members gave me his contribution."

Lindsay washed her hands and took the check. "Well, in that case . . . It will all help, that's sure."

"I'll see if I can't rouse some other support, too," Ben said.

The table had been set in record time, and Gibb took the seat next to Ben's while Beep rummaged in the refrigerator for a glass of juice. "Support for what?" Gibb asked easily.

Before Lindsay could point out that it really wasn't his affair, Ben had told him about the emergency at the shelter for abused women.

"How much do they need?" Gibb asked.

"A couple of thousand would tide them over," Lindsay said reluctantly. "But I'm sure we'll manage. After all, if the plant couldn't afford a contribution yesterday—"

"I'll give you my personal check."

She stared at him, but before she could comment, Beep had wriggled between Gibb and the breakfast bar and was starting to tell him the plot of the last movie he'd seen. Gibb bore the recital patiently, but eventually—at about the middle of the movie—Lindsay took pity on him and interrupted to serve dinner.

The conversation ranged from school to the plant to the party for Gibb, and it carried them through the stir-fry and salad more easily than Lindsay had expected.

As Ben used the last bite of his angel food cake to mop up the remaining strawberry sauce on his plate, he said, "I'll help with the dishes, Beep."

"It's Mom's turn," Beep said. "Besides, I was telling Gibb about the movie, and I want to finish."

"I'll still help with the dishes," Ben said.

Gibb smiled wryly. "Only because you don't want to listen to the rest of the movie." He helped clear the table before Beep dragged him off toward the living room.

Over the sound of running water, Lindsay could hear only bits of the one-sided conversation in the living room. But a little later her ears perked as she heard Gibb say, "You look gloomy all of a sudden."

She looked across the breakfast bar toward them as Beep nodded. "Being grounded is a pain."

"You did the crime, so now you'll have to do the time."

"Yeah, but I just remembered something. I can't..." Beep glanced over his shoulder toward the kitchen and lowered his voice, and Lindsay couldn't catch his words.

I'd better look into that, she thought.

A moment later, she grew even more suspicious when Gibb shook his head firmly. "No, pal. I'm not getting mixed up in that."

"But I can't do it myself," Beep argued.

"You won't be grounded forever."

"No... but somebody else might get there first. And it's *special*."

"Haven't you got me into enough difficulty?" But Gibb's protest wasn't as strong as before, Lindsay thought.

"But it wouldn't be any trouble, really," Beep wheedled.

Lindsay hastily finished wiping the kitchen counter and walked into the living room just as Gibb said, "All right, I'll do it. But you owe me a favor in return."

Beep's face was glowing. "I'll wash your car again."

"If I can stand it," Gibb muttered.

"What are you going to do?" Lindsay asked.

"Just guy stuff, Mom."

"Nothing that will hurt Benjamin," Gibb said. "Or anybody else, either."

There wasn't much she could say; obviously they'd entered a conspiracy of silence. She looked at her watch, then at the clock on the mantel. "Is that the time? My wristwatch must have died this afternoon." And they must have sat over dinner for far longer than she'd realized, as well. "Time for a bath, Beep."

He grumbled for a moment and then said, "Will you run the water? I always get it too hot."

She was just turning off the taps when Beep came into the bathroom. "There," she said. "Just right, I hope. Are you sure you don't want to tell me what that favor is?"

"I'm sure."

"It sounded like some sort of treasure hunt."

Beep gave a throaty chuckle. "Sort of. Yeah."

And that, Lindsay thought, had gotten her precisely nowhere.

Ben and Gibb were in the living room. As she closed the bathroom door she could hear the rumble of masculine voices mixing with the splash of Beep's bathwater.

She closed her eyes in pain. That was the way things should have been, she thought. Her husband and her father relaxing after dinner, her son getting ready for bed.

But it wasn't that way. They had never been a family, and they never could be.

She stood for a couple of minutes in the dim hall, composing herself, and when she went to the living room Ben was gone and Gibb was standing by the front window. He turned as she came in. "Your father said he had some things to do."

I'll bet, Lindsay thought.

"Well—I should be going. I only waited to thank you for the dinner."

"You don't need to rush." She fluffed a sofa pillow and sat down. She ought to tackle him about that favor he'd promised to do for Beep, but something kept her silent. Whatever it was, he'd said it wouldn't hurt Beep or anyone else, and she had no reason to doubt that.

Spats pawed at Gibb's shoe, and he stooped to pick up the animal. The cat twisted around in Gibb's arms till he was comfortable and started to purr so loudly Lindsay had no trouble hearing him across the room.

"Do you like cats?" she asked idly.

Gibb nodded. "And dogs. I can't have one, of course—I'm never in one place long enough, and it wouldn't be fair to an animal to leave it behind."

"Where's home?"

He smiled. "According to my driver's license, it's Denver—but most of the time I go from job to job without getting back there at all."

The picture of such a rootless existence made her want to shiver. "How long have you been doing this?"

"About six years now."

"You must like it."

"There's always a new challenge. I don't get into a rut that way."

Lindsay wondered if the habit of wandering wasn't a kind of rut in itself. "Daddy said you'd been with Triangle from the very beginning. Is that what you did with the money he—" She bit her tongue. "I'm sorry. It's really none of my business."

Gibb nodded. "A couple of friends and I tossed our assets together and bought a little office-supply business that was failing. We brought it back and got a chance to sell it. So we invested the profits in another business...and then we realized that we didn't have to actually buy the company, we could just act as consultants. That was how Triangle started."

"It's obviously been successful." Her voice was husky. "I'm glad, Gibb. I really am happy that things have worked out for you."

He was standing very still, looking at her. Spats, annoyed that the hand that had been so patiently petting him had stilled, pushed his head against Gibb's chin and yowled.

Gibb put him down. "I must be going," he said. "Thanks for dinner, Lindsay. It was very good."

She went to the staircase with him. "Not quite like the old days," she said, and laughed a little at how hopeless her cooking had been back then.

He turned, and in the dimness at the top of the stairs, she didn't realize what he intended until his lips brushed lightly against her cheek. "I'm sorry I couldn't be what you needed, Lindsay," he said very quietly.

She stood there for a long time, with her hand cupped over her cheek. She was still there when Beep came out of the bathroom wearing only a towel. His hair was still wet and he left damp footprints across the oak floor.

He stopped in the middle of the room and said, sounding outraged, "Gibb's gone? But I wanted him to tuck me in!"

"Maybe he didn't realize that." She helped to dry his hair, then put him to bed. "You must remember Gibb's not your personal property, Beep."

"I know. But..." He yawned. "Do you think he'd like to come to my soccer games?"

"You may ask."

He cast a sidelong glance at her. "He could sit with you. I know how bored you get sometimes."

"Hold it right there, Benjamin. He who gets caught up in his own power sometimes gets a shock."

"Huh?"

"It's an ancient Chinese proverb that I just made up. It means, don't try to manipulate your mother." She kissed his forehead and went to the living room.

Elementary school soccer games *were* on the dull side. But that was no reason to be picturing herself in the stands with Gibb beside her.

"What is the matter with me?" Lindsay muttered. The man had lied to her and walked out on her. Why on earth, then, did she find herself thinking about him as anything more than a painful memory?

Or *had* he lied to her? He'd told her he didn't want children. Was it his fault that a younger and more idealistic Lindsay hadn't believed until that final quarrel that he meant it? And he hadn't walked out on her so much as she'd thrown him out. It had been an inevitable end, of course; it was only a matter of time, and if Lindsay hadn't made the break, Gibb no doubt would have.

But despite it all—all the pain, all the harsh memories, all the years when she had tried to forget...

"I wish he was coming home to me," she whispered.

Her heart was pounding suddenly, as if actually saying the words had given life to the feelings. But that wasn't true, she knew; those emotions had lain deeply buried within her since he'd left. She had carefully placed a veneer of calm over them, and pretended they were no longer valid—but she had never stopped caring. And as soon as he had come back, those feelings had begun to stir.

That was why it had hurt so much yesterday when he'd kissed her. She had hurt so badly because she had wanted that kiss to mean something to Gibb—as it had to her. He'd wakened a hunger inside her, but it had found no answering need in him.

That was why she'd been so wounded when she heard the distaste in his voice afterward, when he'd said that only a fool would make business decisions based on physical attraction. Though she wasn't so sure he'd felt even that much. He'd kissed her to make a point, that was all.

And tonight, when she'd told him she was happy for him, he'd walked away. She meant so little to him that he didn't even want her good wishes.

She ought to be furious with him—or at least offended. But in fact, all she felt was sadness, and the deep, aching soul hunger of a love that—unlike her marriage—had never died.

CHAPTER EIGHT

LINDSAY had never been so beautiful as when she was sitting in that dimly lighted living room, Gibb thought. Her face, in the soft yellow glow of the lamps, had been almost tender, and the husky undertone of her voice had been like the softly haunting music of an oboe.

He was absolutely furious that she still had the power to attract him—that she could take his self-control in those small, delicate hands and rip it to shreds as easily as she'd destroy a cobweb. She hadn't even done anything to cause that attraction. He was convinced that the sensual magnetism she had exuded had been completely subconscious. But simply seeing her sitting there, nestled into the soft cushions of that deep couch, her body warm and relaxed, had set his blood aflame. He'd had a choice then. He could walk out, or he could pick her up and carry her to her bedroom and explore the possibility that once more the immense power of their lovemaking could shut out everything else in the world.

For a long, long moment, he had wavered—and that, too, had made him angry. It had terrified him, as well, for he had no right to be her lover now. So he had left—but it had taken every bit of his waning self-discipline.

He had no right to want her, and he knew that in the long run he would only be fooling himself if he persisted. The physical attraction they had once shared had not been enough to overcome the chasm that lay between them nine years ago, and nothing that had happened since had made that chasm any easier to bridge.

In fact, if anything, it was wider now, for there was her child—the son who stood between them and made it utterly impossible that they could ever recapture the glow of those early weeks of marriage, when it was enough just to be together.

Benjamin was a nice enough kid, as kids went. Gibb had no trouble admitting that. But being around a child for an afternoon was one thing, while taking one on for life—

The thought made him shudder to the depths of his soul. It was impossible, and that was all there was to it.

And if being around Lindsay was going to soften his brain like this, it would be far better to simply stay away.

I really am happy that things have worked out for you, she'd said. Well, dammit, he didn't want her to be happy for him. He wanted her to miss him—

No. That was silly, stupid, even selfish. Even if she did miss him, even if she still cared, it was impossible that there could ever be anything between them again. There was the child.

The child who should have been his—but wasn't. The very idea that Benjamin might have been his son, had things been different, sent chills down Gibb's spine.

No, he'd keep his distance from them both.

Except, he reminded himself irritably, that he'd made a couple of foolish promises he couldn't go back on.

Being without her wristwatch over the weekend nearly drove Lindsay crazy. But she had no help in the store on Monday, so it was late afternoon before she could escape long enough to run across the square to Henderson's Jewelry to have it fixed.

She was almost to the service department window when she realized that the tall man standing at the cash register was Gibb. He obviously saw her at the same instant, and in one smooth motion he flipped shut the little velvet-covered box that lay on the counter beside him and slid it into his pocket.

She hadn't seen the contents; he'd moved too fast for that. A magician would have been proud of the expert sleight of hand, Lindsay thought. But she knew it had been a small, square red velvet box. Precisely the size to hold a diamond ring.

She told herself that just because a man patronized an upscale jewelry store didn't mean he was buying diamonds. But she couldn't help remembering Skye's earnest voice saying, "Gibb and I have become very close." Or that wisecrack of Ian Russell's at Kathy's party, about the only proper follow-up to a lobster dinner at the Willows being an engagement.

Of course, she reminded herself, there was also what Gibb himself had said about not being cut out for marriage. But perhaps there was something about Skye that made him willing to try again. Something, obviously, that was very different from Lindsay...

Don't jump to conclusions, she told herself. Just because that box *could* hold a diamond ring didn't mean it *did*.

But whatever Gibb had purchased, it was certainly for Skye—why else would he have hidden it in his pocket and looked just a little frozen at the sight of Lindsay?

Jealousy gnawed at her stomach. It was one thing to admit intellectually that their marriage was long over and Gibb was perfectly free to enter another relationship. But it was something else to stand by and watch it happen, and wonder what was different now and precisely what it was about the new woman in his life that had apparently restored his faith.

You don't know that's what's going on, Lindsay reminded herself. Nevertheless, it was as much as she could do to smile and greet him and walk by to hand her watch to the repairman. "It's only a dead battery, I think," she told him.

The sales clerk finished ringing up Gibb's purchase. Despite her resolution to ignore the transaction, Lindsay couldn't keep herself from turning around just enough to see what was going on. She was heartily ashamed of herself, but she couldn't help realizing that if the clerk counted out Gibb's change aloud, she could calculate how much he'd spent. And, she had to admit, she wanted to know.

But he must have written a check, for there was no change, just a flatteringly eager expression of gratitude for his business. Which indicated, Lindsay thought dryly, that it had probably been a purchase of some size. At least, she'd never gotten that kind of thanks at Henderson's for buying a watch battery.

Gibb folded his receipt and tucked it safely in his wallet, then came across to the service window. "Are you going back to the shop?" he asked.

Automatically Lindsay checked her wrist, looking for the time, and sighed when once more she found it bare. "I'll be there as soon as my watch is fixed."

"I'll stop by for a moment, if I may. I've got something for you."

Lindsay nodded, and he went out. She almost forgot to pay for her purchase because she was so confused. What could he have for her?

Then she remembered the check he'd promised for the crisis shelter. That made sense; he wouldn't want to hand that over to just anyone.

But when Gibb came into Potpourri a few minutes later, he was carrying an enormous plastic bag. It didn't look heavy, just a bit awkward because of its size, and Lindsay hurried to push Beep's homework aside on the big table behind the cash register so Gibb could set the package down.

Beep closed his spelling book without a second's hesitation and grinned at Gibb. "Boy, am I glad to see you. You know that bike chain I broke the other day? I've been trying to fix it, but I think I lost a piece."

"Don't bother Gibb," Lindsay told him. "You can't ride the bike for weeks anyway, remember?"

Gibb was watching her intently—as if, Lindsay thought, he'd like to argue once more that Beep's punishment was too severe. She put her chin up a trifle and met his gaze.

As if she'd issued a challenge, Gibb said, "I don't suppose it will hurt to have a look." He pointed to the package. "Go ahead and open that, Lindsay."

But he didn't wait for her to do so. He and Beep went off toward the storeroom and the bicycle.

Lindsay shrugged and opened the bag. It was stuffed with brand-new towels—far more of them than Gibb and Beep had used on Saturday to wash the car. There were towels of all sizes and shapes, and matching washcloths, all in the best quality of velour and exactly the dark, clear jewel colors that hers had been before they'd been subjected to wax and chrome polish.

There were so many towels, in fact, that they spilled over the edges of the table and onto the floor. Lindsay looked helplessly at the mess and told herself firmly that it was a very thoughtful thing for Gibb to do.

But under the surface, she was seething with anger and jealous rage.

She knew she wasn't being fair. But she couldn't help the comparison that filled her mind. For Skye, he had bought jewelry. Lindsay could almost picture a solitaire diamond winking on a slender gold band inside that red velvet box, which was probably resting in his pocket right now. While for Lindsay, he'd punctiliously shopped for towels to replace the ones he'd ruined . . .

Towels! She'd like to choke him with one of them.

The last thing Lindsay wanted to do was go to the welcoming party for Gibb on Sunday afternoon. She postponed getting ready as long as she could, and when Dave Jonas called and asked her to go to the movie matinee with him, she hesitated before she said, "I can't, Dave. I've got to go to a ghastly party."

"Can't you make a token appearance and cut out? It's a really good show."

The idea was appealing. Any movie would no doubt be more fun than watching Skye Oliver simper over Gibb. And if the woman happened to be wearing a new diamond ring . . .

Impulsively, Lindsay said, "Why don't you come to the party, Dave? It's the Courthouse Squares, so you know everybody—and Mrs. Johnson won't mind an extra. Besides, if you're right there, maybe it'll be easier to make my excuses and fade away."

Dave agreed to pick her up in a few minutes, and Lindsay put the phone down. Beep was watching her intently from the kitchen table, where he was putting together a jigsaw puzzle. "Can I go?" he asked. "I'm a Courthouse Square, too."

"Adults only, I'm afraid."

He stuck out his lower lip. "What kind of a party is it?"

"A dull one. Tea and talk, that's all."

"Talk about what? Things like how bad Mr. Johnson's knees are hurting today?"

"That's exactly what I mean."

"Oh." He snapped in another piece. "I guess I'll stay home, then. I like the kind of party that has a clown or games or presents."

"Oh, heavens, I forgot about that." What was she going to give Gibb as a housewarming gift? Some item that was small and fun—wasn't that what Mrs. Johnson had suggested? Lindsay couldn't skip a gift altogether; that would cause comment from the other guests. But she'd have to be careful what it was, too, or there'd be just as much talk.

Beep had started in again. "If the party is only for the Squares, how come you invited Dave?"

Lindsay wasn't quite sure of that herself. The invitation had been no more than a spur-of-the-moment whim, and it would probably lead to all kinds of renewed speculation about her intentions where Dave was concerned. Had she simply given in to a Freudian urge to show Gibb that her love life hadn't come to a dead halt, any more than his had?

"Dave's not a Courthouse Square," Beep went on, "so—"

"Beep, believe me, you'll have more fun here with Heidi than you would at the party."

His lip stuck out even farther. "Why did you call Heidi, anyway?"

"Because I couldn't get your regular sitter."

"I'm too big for a baby-sitter."

"I know you're convinced of that. But if you think I'm going off to a party and leave you here alone—"

"You'll only be across the square."

"That's right. And with Heidi keeping you company, I'll know that you're safe. I'll be back in a couple of hours, anyway. A token appearance at the party and a short movie—"

"Two hours? That's hardly even enough time to watch a video."

"Are you complaining? Want me to stay out longer?"

"Oh, Mom. I just mean I'd be perfectly all right on my own for two lousy hours in the middle of the afternoon."

"Well, two hours may be hardly enough time for a video, but it's plenty of time to get into trouble—and you are still grounded. End of argument, Beep."

He sighed. "Will Gibb be at the party? He's a Courthouse Square now."

"Probably." It was close enough to the truth, and Lindsay knew if she told Beep that the party was actually in Gibb's honor, he'd really throw a fit about missing it.

"Why hasn't Gibb been back to see us all week?"

"He's busy, I suppose. I think there have been some difficulties at the plant."

"I miss him."

"I know. But I guess you'll have to get used to it." Lindsay saw the hurt in Beep's eyes and had to steel herself against it. Better a small wound now than a bigger one later, she reminded herself. The less fanciful his dreams about Gibb became, the easier it would be when he bumped up against reality—as he'd inevitably have to do. "Gibb won't be here much longer anyway, I expect. As soon as the mess at the plant is straightened out, he'll go on to his next job."

Beep looked as if he'd like to argue the point, but to Lindsay's relief, the teenage sitter rang the bell just then.

"Go let Heidi in, will you, honey?" she said, and went to get the soft wool jacket that matched her tailored trousers.

When Beep came upstairs, not only the sitter was following him, but Dave, as well. He kissed Lindsay's cheek lightly, and she said, "That was fast."

"I figured, why waste any more time on the party than necessary? Get there first and get out."

She smiled. "Heidi, I'm sorry to do this to you, but since Beep's grounded, I'm afraid his activities are limited."

"That's bad news, fella," the sitter said. "I thought maybe you'd like to go to the park, but I suppose that's out."

"You're right," Lindsay said. "Regular television rules, and there are snacks in the refrigerator for both of you. I'll be home right after the movie. Be good, all right?" She kissed the top of Beep's head and ran her fingers through her hair, spreading it evenly over the collar of her jacket, then turned to Dave. "I still need a gift, but I guess I'll just have to grab something from the shop."

"You didn't tell me there were going to be presents," Beep grumbled.

"Probably nothing you'd think was worthwhile. Don't make Heidi's life miserable, okay?" Lindsay didn't wait for an answer.

She stopped at the bottom of the stairs and looked around the storeroom with something close to desperation. Most of the merchandise she carried was more ornamental than useful, and she couldn't quite see Gibb carefully packing up that sort of thing to carry around the country with him. Music boxes were too delicate for that kind of treatment. A potpourri bowl could be interpreted as a wish for him to remember both her store and Lindsay herself. He would have little use for anything crystal or china, and candles were such a feminine touch. A picture frame, maybe? He could always put a photograph of Skye in it.

Lindsay's gaze fell on a patch of purple and green on the storeroom shelf, and she remembered the garish hairpin lace afghan. The young woman who'd made it had come in last week and promised to make another sample, in colors of Lindsay's choosing, so she'd left the brilliant one out of sight. She figured that in a month or two, when she'd sold a few, she'd give it back; she had no idea what else she'd ever do with it.

But there was something that tickled her sense of humor about giving that horrible afghan to Gibb. And after all, it was a housewarming. What could be warmer than a soft wool afghan to bundle up in?

"I'll just be a minute," she told Dave. She grabbed a box from the pile stored under the stairs, laid the afghan carefully in it and went into the shop to the gift-wrap area.

He followed. "What's the deal?"

"Oh, the party's for Gibb—just a little housewarming affair."

Dave didn't say anything for half a minute, and by the time he spoke, Lindsay had the bundle neatly folded in brilliant paper. "In that case, maybe I shouldn't go."

Lindsay taped the package. "Are things at the plant getting that bad?"

"They're not any worse, exactly, but everybody's tense. Gardner's watching everything that goes on, all the production steps and every machine, till it's making all the employees so nervous they could scream. And he's starting to interview people, too."

"Prospective employees, you mean? But isn't that good? If he's thinking of hiring—"

Dave shook his head. "That's not what I mean. He's talking to the ones who already work there—calling them into his office one or two at a time."

Lindsay was puzzled. "Well, that's not so unreasonable, is it?"

"If he was asking about their jobs, no. But it's just chitchat—as if he doesn't really care about the subject because he's only fulfilling an obligation to talk to everyone before he lays them off."

The gift wrap ripped under Lindsay's nails. "Oh, Dave—"

"It's only a suspicion," he added hastily. "If you know anything, Lindsay..."

"I don't. I'm sorry, but nobody's been telling me anything." She patched up the tear in the paper and finished the package with an enormous white bow. "Let's go and get this party over with."

They walked across the square to the Johnsons' apartment, on the floor above an insurance agency's office. They'd installed an elevator in the building because of Mr. Johnson's knees, so Lindsay and Dave rode up in state. As Lindsay rang the bell, she noticed the apartment was silent except for a vague rustle. The stillness nagged at her; this was hardly the atmosphere she'd expect for a party, even the quiet sort the Courthouse Squares preferred.

The door opened just as she was starting to wonder if she'd mistaken the time, and Mrs. Johnson ushered them into the empty living room.

"Are we too early?" Lindsay asked.

With blinding suddenness, a couple of dozen people poured in from the adjoining rooms, with shouts of "Surprise!" and "Happy birthday, Lindsay!"

Lindsay was stunned. She clutched the package containing the afghan and stared at the enthusiastic group of neighbors who crowded around. "But it's more than two weeks till my birthday."

Mrs. Johnson started to laugh. "Well, I guess I showed everybody who thought we couldn't manage to surprise you! You really didn't suspect, did you, Lindsay? I thought you wouldn't, if we had the party early and told you it was another kind of event altogether. Wasn't it sweet of Mr. Gardner to play along and let you think the party was for him?"

Lindsay hadn't seen Gibb until then. He must have come in with the crowd, but he'd stayed apart from them, sitting on the arm of a chair and looking a bit bored.

Sweet? That was about the last adjective she'd use to describe Gibb Gardner, and Lindsay had to gulp hard before she could nod a polite agreement.

"But I must say," Mrs. Johnson went on, "when you suggested we make it a housewarming with gifts for him, I had all I could do not to burst out laughing. Do come on in, dear, and enjoy your party." She urged Lindsay toward a tea table set up across the room and thrust a crystal plate into her hand.

Behind the table was Skye Oliver, holding a knife poised over the corner of an enormous decorated cake. She was looking a little sullen, Lindsay thought, and wondered when Mrs. Johnson had broken the news to her that the party wasn't for Gibb, after all.

Lindsay managed to hang back long enough to ask Dave, "Did you know about this?"

He looked astounded. "Of course not. I wanted to see the movie—and I suppose there isn't a prayer we'll get out of here in time."

"I'm sorry, Dave. Go ahead, if you like. I don't mind."

"Oh, no—I'm not such a poor sport as that. For better, for worse, for parties...you know, all that stuff."

The careless phrase made Lindsay uneasy, and she saw Skye's gaze sharpen. But there wasn't time to worry about it then, so she took the piece of cake Skye offered and a cup of tea, and made up her mind to enjoy her party.

Everyone had brought small presents—some thoughtful, some teasing. Gibb had given her a gift certificate to the Willows; Lindsay awarded him points for finding a token in which no one could find hidden meanings.

She exclaimed over each trinket, and when the pile was finished and only one package—the one she herself had brought—remained, she glanced at it and sighed. She could hardly pick the darned thing up and take it home with her, so she looked across the room at Gibb and said lightly, "You might as well have your house-warming gift anyway."

Neither reluctant nor eager, he opened the package, carefully slitting the tape and unfolding the paper. He'd never ripped packages; Lindsay had almost forgotten how annoyed she used to get at the time he'd take over the smallest and simplest of gifts. It was almost as if he savored the crackle of the paper, the slickness of the bow—as if the package was more important than the contents.

Skye leaned over his chair to watch, and for the first time Lindsay got a good look at the woman's left hand.

The ring finger was bare, and relief surged through Lindsay's veins for a moment before she got control of herself once more. How stupid it was to think that whatever Gibb did mattered to her!

Except it did matter. It was very important, indeed.

She hadn't wanted to come to the party—not because she didn't want to see Gibb, but because she was afraid of what she would feel when she faced him again.

All week she had been telling herself that what she felt now was only a faint echo stirred to life by his presence, and that it would fade once more into silence as soon as he was gone. She had tried to convince herself that what she had experienced on the night they had sat together in the twilight of her living room had been only the dregs that any woman would feel when confronted with a man she had once cared for. But despite that flare of feeling, she had told herself, her love was nine years dead.

As long as she hadn't seen him face to face, Lindsay could almost convince herself that she was telling the truth. But the moment she was in the same room with him, she could feel the magnetism of the man; all her pretenses drained away, and she was left to face the naked truth.

She loved him. She always had, and she always would. The disagreement that had shattered their marriage had not had the power to destroy her love.

Skye looked into the box at the brilliant afghan. "I suppose you chose the colors yourself, Lindsay?" she drawled. "How perfectly charming of you to try to keep Gibb warm."

Someone else said, in an undertone, "It'll keep him *awake*, that's sure!"

"Let's get on with the party, shall we?" Gibb put the lid on the box and set it aside. "You're very thoughtful, Lindsay."

"Isn't she?" Skye murmured. "She's doing her very best to make you feel at home. Terrifying, isn't it?"

Lindsay bit her tongue, then set her pile of gifts aside and went to fill her teacup. There was nothing to be gained by getting into a cat-scratching contest with Skye.

Someone started to tease Gibb about opening a car wash at the battery plant. "It might even improve the profit-and-loss statement," he said, "especially if you hire that kid of Lindsay's. He looks like a cheap and enthusiastic worker."

Gibb only smiled.

Skye followed Lindsay to the tea table. "You'd like that, wouldn't you?"

"I don't know what you mean."

"Having your kid in Gibb's pocket. That's why you sent him over there to visit, isn't it?"

Lindsay was startled. "Beep's been visiting Gibb?"

"Oh, don't play innocent. It was obviously your idea." Skye set her cup down with a crash and turned on her heel.

Since when had Beep been visiting Gibb? Not this week, that was sure—he'd been under Lindsay's feet all the time and grumbling because he *hadn't* seen Gibb. But suddenly those grumbles took on new meaning. If he'd been visiting Gibb before he was grounded ...

Lindsay didn't know what to think.

The discussion of the car wash had worn itself out, and the talk had turned more serious. "I don't want to put you on the spot, Gibb," Mr. Johnson said, "but there's a rumor going around that Armentrout stock won't pay dividends this quarter."

The humor had died out of Gibb's face, leaving a tight wariness about the eyes. "That's not the only rumor that's flying," he said. "But as soon as there's anything definite—about dividends or anything else—there will be an announcement."

He hadn't denied the possibility, Lindsay realized. Shocked, she stared across the room at him. For the moment, Beep was forgotten.

Eliminating the investors' dividends—or even cutting them back—would be like running a knife across the throat of the entire company. A business that wasn't paying back its investors would find it difficult—maybe impossible—to raise capital for the kind of changes or expansions the plant would need to be efficient once more. To make such a move would be admitting defeat.

Lindsay stood beside the tea table, almost stunned, until the murmurs had died down. Gibb made no explanation, and finally the conversation turned to another subject.

Only then did she make her way quietly across the room to stand beside Gibb's chair. "You can't do that," she said, low-voiced.

"Why not? Though I understand your concern. I see from the stockholders' listings that Armentrout dividends must be the major source of your income."

"Dammit, Gibb, do you think I'm that selfish?" But he was correct about her income, and the implications were only starting to hit her. Potpourri supported itself and turned a small profit, but it wasn't enough to live on. And she had just last week ordered more Christmas merchandise than ever before, because she'd had such a good season last year. Without her regular dividend income, how would she pay for that merchandise when it arrived?

"I wish you'd never come back here," she said. Her voice was almost lifeless.

"I'm only the bearer of bad news, Lindsay, not the cause of it. The plant was in trouble long before I came."

She shook her head, more in sadness than disagreement.

"I told you once that if you really want me out of town, there's one way I can speed things up."

"I remember," Lindsay said acidly. "You'll close the plant and sell off the pieces."

Gibb nodded. "Of course, then there would never be any more dividends, would there?"

Lindsay hadn't seen Dave Jonas come up beside her. "And you'd like that, wouldn't you, Gardner?" Venom seemed to drip from Dave's voice. "Crushing the whole plant, and most of the town, would be a fitting way to get even. How long are you going to keep us hanging before you drop the ax?"

The room had gone totally silent. Lindsay thought, almost hysterically, that it looked something like an old-fashioned tableau—a frozen pantomime.

Mr. Johnson moved eventually, to put a hand on Dave's shoulder. "It's a party, son," he said. "Let's have a good time."

But the fun had gone from the afternoon, and not long afterward the Courthouse Squares started making their excuses. Gibb was among the last to leave; Lindsay thought perhaps he felt he had to stay or be accused of running away.

By the time she'd gathered up her gifts and helped restore order to the Johnsons' apartment, it was too late for the movie. Dave walked Lindsay across the square, carrying a box full of her birthday gifts.

"Beep's going to be really upset when he sees this," she said. "The very idea of having a birthday party and not inviting him will send him straight up the wall."

Dave grunted.

"I'm sorry," she said. "I know you wanted to see the movie."

He shook his head. "That's not what's bothering me. This thing with Gardner and the plant... Dammit, Lindsay, you do understand, don't you?"

"Understand what?" she asked carefully.

"I'd love to propose to you, but as long as everything's so uncertain at the plant—"

It had been a day full of shocks, but somehow this one was the final blow. "Please, Dave," she said helplessly. "Don't."

"That's just it, honey. I can't. I know it's pretty tacky of me to bring the subject up at all, under the circumstances, but till I know if I've got a job—"

Lindsay's head was swimming. She couldn't turn down an offer that hadn't been made. Yet to say nothing would leave Dave feeling that she would welcome a proposal eventually—and that would be horribly unfair.

But before she could say anything at all, he saw the expression in her eyes and released an explosive sigh. "So that's the way the wind blows, is it? You still care about him, don't you?"

Yes, her heart said. But the instinct to protect herself made her temporize. "I don't know, Dave. I'm so confused."

"You and the rest of the town," he said gloomily. He stopped at the edge of the little courtyard and handed her the box of gifts.

"Would you like to come up for coffee?"

Dave considered and shook his head. "I don't think so. I'll see you around, Lindsay."

She watched him out of sight around the corner of the building, and crossed the little patio to the back door. The box wasn't heavy, but it was a bit awkward, and she had to balance it in order to turn the dials of the combination lock. She didn't notice the piece of paper stuck in the narrow crack between door and jamb until the lock clicked open. The paper—a note from the sitter, perhaps?—fluttered to the ground and skittered off across the tiles.

Lindsay had to set the box down in order to chase the paper, and she said a couple of words that she usually reserved for moments of high stress. Hadn't she made it perfectly clear to Heidi that Beep was confined to the building? Where could they have gone, anyway?

But the note wasn't from the sitter. It was a plain sheet of white paper, half covered with words cut from newspaper and magazine headlines of various sizes and styles. The words were terse, simple and to the point—three blunt sentences that tore her world apart and turned it upside down.

We've got the kid, it said. *No cops or you'll be sorry. Wait for directions.*

The note slid from her nerveless fingers, and the breeze caught it and whirled it away. With her heart in her mouth, Lindsay snatched the fluttering paper, and only when it was clutched once more in her hand did she realize that it wasn't even addressed to her.

Instead, on the outside of the folded page in the same sort of large and irregular capitals, Gibb's name was spelled out.

Her son had been kidnapped—but it seemed Gibb would be the one asked to pay the ransom.

CHAPTER NINE

LINDSAY'S chest ached; every effort to draw a breath sent agonizing pain shooting like hot knives up through her shoulders and down through her abdomen. Was this what it felt like to have a heart attack?

Beep was gone.

Don't be a fool, she told herself. She didn't even know there was anything wrong at all. Beep might very well be upstairs with Heidi, exactly where he was supposed to be. The note might be someone's idea of a prank. A sick, venomous, hateful practical joke—but perhaps no closer than that to truth.

If anything, the fact that the note was addressed to Gibb made that possibility more likely. With everything that was going on at the plant, perhaps someone had chosen this horrible way to make a point.

It wouldn't take a genius to figure out that threatening Gibb wouldn't have much effect, for the half-formed warning Dave had told her about hadn't changed a thing in the way Gibb approached the business.

But to threaten a child, a child who bore Gibb's name and who was Ben Armentrout's grandson...

Everybody in town knew how fond Ben was of his only grandchild. He'd put any amount of pressure on Gibb to pay the price—whatever it might be—to get Beep safely back. And everybody in town also seemed to know that Gibb had been spending time with Beep. If the people who had made the threat believed that Beep was

149

his son after all, then they might think it wouldn't take much persuasion to get what they wanted from Gibb.

Lindsay swallowed hard. The wind had picked up and turned chilly, and it cut through her wool jacket. Or was she suddenly so cold because her blood had frozen with fear? She was afraid to go upstairs, terrified of what she would find—and yet not knowing was almost worse.

It was a good thing she'd already unlocked the door, because her fingers were shaking too hard to move the dial to the right combination. She almost fell as she crossed the storeroom and plunged up the stairs. She was trying desperately to keep her panic under control, but without much success. She hadn't felt like this since the time Beep had fallen off the top of a stone wall and she thought he'd fractured his skull.

But this terror was even worse.

The moment she reached the top of the stairs, she called sharply, "Beep!"

There was no answer—nothing at all. Was Heidi gone, too?

Lindsay had to strain her eyes to see the length of the apartment, for twilight had fallen, and the drapes in the living room area had been drawn. The only light at the front of the apartment came from the unsteady flicker of the television screen. Everything seemed to be in place. Lindsay could see no sign anywhere of a struggle.

She took a deep breath and started across the room, fearful of what she might see on the floor where the couch blocked her view. "Heidi?" Her voice cracked with fear.

The teenager sat up, yawning, and swung her legs off the couch. She flipped her long hair over her shoulder and said casually, "Oh, hi, Mrs. G. Sorry—I must have fallen asleep. It was a pretty dull video. You're home early, aren't you?''

"No," Lindsay said tautly. "I'm not early at all. Where's Beep?''

The girl looked around vaguely. "Isn't he in his room?''

Lindsay bit back sharp words, turned on her heel and went down the hall.

The big red kite was hanging on a hook behind Beep's bedroom door. A dog-eared comic book poked out from under his pillow. His schoolbooks were stacked on the corner of his desk. On a shelf was the stuffed elephant that had comforted him in his crib, so worn now that most of the fur was gone.

But Beep wasn't there. The empty room echoed the hollowness in Lindsay's stomach.

Heidi trailed down the hall to the door. "Golly, I thought sure he'd be back by now.''

Lindsay wheeled on her. "*Back*? What do you mean, back?''

The teenager shrugged. "He wanted a pack of gum from the drugstore, so I let him go. I must have gone to sleep while he was gone, but I thought he'd only be a minute.''

But instead someone had been waiting for him, or had spotted him and seized the opportunity.

Bile rose in Lindsay's throat, and it was all she could do not to smack the girl across the face for her carelessness. "I told you he wasn't allowed to leave the building!''

Heidi shook her head. "Not exactly. You said he couldn't go to the park because he was grounded. But you've always let him go out on the square by himself, so I thought it couldn't hurt.''

Heidi had not followed her instructions—but she was right about one thing, and Lindsay had to admit it. As soon as Beep had learned to cross streets safely, she'd allowed him to have the run of the square. If he hadn't been grounded, she herself would have allowed him to walk down the block to the drugstore without a second thought. In a little town like Elmwood, what could go wrong?

The innocence of the question left a sour taste in her mouth.

She thrust the note at Heidi, who read it and turned pale. "You mean somebody grabbed him on the way to the drugstore?"

"It doesn't look as if he's here, does it?" Lindsay said bitterly. "When did he go, Heidi? How long has he been gone?"

The girl looked at the bedside alarm clock. "About an hour," she admitted.

"An *hour*? They could have taken him anywhere by now. And you were asleep." Lindsay swallowed the rest of the accusation. It was pointless to flay the girl now. In the end, the responsibility belonged to Lindsay; she was the one who had hired Heidi and entrusted Beep to her care.

"I'm sorry, Mrs. G. I had a late date last night, and..." Heidi's voice trailed off, as she realized that no excuse was good enough and that Lindsay wasn't listening anyway.

Lindsay had to look up the Olivers' phone number, and between shaking fingers and blurry eyes she tried three times to dial it before she got it right.

Just hearing Gibb's deep voice brought a flood of tears. There was something so terribly solid about him.

"Gibb, Beep's gone," she wailed.

"What? Gone? You mean he's run away?"

She sniffed hard. "No. He's been kidnapped."

There was a momentary pause. "Oh, come on, Lindsay. In Elmwood? He probably got tired of being grounded and just took off to teach you a lesson."

"Beep would never do that. And there's a note, Gibb."

The sudden silence at the other end of the telephone was thick and tense. It comforted her a little to know that the news had hit Gibb hard, too.

"It's addressed to you," she added drearily.

"I'll be right over." All the life had drained out of Gibb's voice.

Lindsay put the phone down and absently rubbed her nose with the back of her hand. She was still standing in the same spot when Gibb came up the stairs; it could have been only a matter of minutes, but it seemed aeons to Lindsay.

He set a box on the kitchen table. "You left the back door open, and this was sitting on the step."

She shivered at the sight of the birthday gifts. Had it only been an hour ago that she'd been opening them, exclaiming in delight at every one? It must have been at the same moment Beep was being lured away or bodily carried off. Had he been terrified? Had he tried to escape? Had they hurt him?

Shudders shook her body, and she hugged her arms tight across her chest.

"Tell me about it." Gibb put a hand on her cheek, and suddenly it felt perfectly natural to go into his arms, to huddle there as if he could protect her from the horror. She buried her face in his cashmere sweater.

"It's my fault," she mumbled against his shoulder, "for leaving him with Heidi. I couldn't get my regular sitter today." She drew a quivering breath. "But I've used Heidi before, and everything was fine—"

Gibb gave her a little shake. "Come on, Lindsay, let's be reasonable. Calm down. You can't do Beep any good by having hysterics."

"Would you slap me if I did?" She was only half-conscious of the question.

"If I had to," he said grimly, "so let's not make it necessary, all right? You said there was a note? Have you read it?"

Lindsay nodded. "I didn't realize at first that it was addressed to you. I think I put it on the table."

Gibb squeezed her shoulders lightly and let her go. He picked the paper up by the very corners, and Lindsay could almost see the words carving themselves on his brain, just as they had on hers, as he read the three terse sentences. Then he set the page down and looked at her. "Why would anybody take Benjamin? And why would they drag me into it?"

Lindsay shook her head. "I don't know. I suppose it might be somebody at the plant—"

"Your friend Dave Jonas, perhaps?"

"No!"

Gibb's eyes narrowed. "Why not?" he asked practically. "He's the one who told you about the threats against me—maybe he's the one who made them. He hasn't exactly been supportive of the idea of change."

"He was with me this afternoon. Remember? Heidi says Beep's been gone about an hour, and Dave was right there in the Johnsons' living room."

"But the question is, why was he there? He doesn't live on the square, does he?"

"No," Lindsay admitted.

"Then whose idea was it for him to come to the party?"

"Mine. He called this afternoon to ask me to a movie, and I suggested he come with me instead."

"He could have planned it, so he wouldn't be suspected," Gibb said thoughtfully. "Taking you to a movie would get you out of the way and give him an alibi. The party was no different, really."

She was furious. "What do you have against Dave?"

"Oh, for one thing, that little outburst this afternoon. It didn't exactly put him on my side, you know."

"He wouldn't have said anything of the sort if he was involved in this, Gibb. He'd know it would cause suspicion."

"Maybe. But would he care? If he had his alibi already in place—"

"You can't have it both ways, Gibb. If he was brilliant enough to arrange an alibi, he wouldn't have blown up at you."

"I'm not so sure. But that's an argument we can't afford just now." He looked at the ransom note without touching it. "This doesn't look like a professional job, Lindsay."

"You know so much about kidnapping?"

"Use your head. It took a lot of cutting and pasting to create the note. There must be layers of fingerprints on this paper."

Lindsay bit her lip unhappily. "Oh."

"I suppose that means yours are included?" Gibb said dryly.

Her voice was defensive. "I didn't know it was important. The note was just stuck in the door, and it blew away. When I caught it—" She gulped. "I sort of crumpled it. Then Heidi read it—"

"Oh, great." He turned to Heidi as she came into the kitchen. "Want to tell me what happened?"

Her face twisted. "I don't know, exactly. He wanted a pack of gum, and the drugstore's only two doors down the street. He said he'd go right there and come straight back. So I let him go." She burst into sobs. "How was I supposed to know?"

Lindsay's gaze met Gibb's. It was obvious, he seemed to be saying, that they'd get nothing more out of Heidi for a while.

"Have you called the police yet?" Gibb asked.

"No. The note says no cops."

"Look, Lindsay—"

The last thread of her composure snapped. "I want my son back! I don't care what you have to do, just get him back!"

Gibb said quietly, "I'm trying to do exactly that, Lindsay, and the best way to begin is to call the police chief and start a quiet investigation."

She bit her lip. "All right." Her voice cracked.

"And somebody should call Ben. If you don't feel up to it..."

Lindsay shook her head. "You do it." She couldn't bear to tell the story again herself, and she didn't think she could stand there and listen, either. She wandered toward the bedrooms, and when Gibb came to find her a little later, she was standing in the hallway clutching Beep's elephant.

"The chief's arranging a tap on this phone and putting observers in the courthouse tower," he said quietly, and Lindsay nodded. "He'll be over to get the note as soon as he finishes his phone calls. And your father is on his way. In the meantime, do you mind if I look around the building?"

"Why? They wouldn't have hidden him here."

He hesitated for the barest fraction of an instant. "It's something to do to keep me busy."

"I don't care. Look all you like."

He turned toward Beep's room.

Suddenly things dropped into place in Lindsay's mind, and the threadbare coat of the stuffed elephant ripped under her nails. "Wait, Gibb. You think he might still be here, don't you? You think he might be..." She swallowed hard. "Dead."

Gibb wouldn't meet her eyes. "It'll be all right," he said. But there was no conviction in his voice.

On the night he'd been invited to dinner, Gibb hadn't gone past the living room of Lindsay's apartment. But there was no doubt at all about which bedroom was Beep's—there were cartoon characters on the sheets and curtains, a neatly framed star map on one wall and a bright red kite hanging behind the door. He could see Lindsay's touch in every inch. A little boy's haven, the room was a private space any child could take delight in—nice, but not so elegant that it was uncomfortable, and just messy enough to be inviting.

Gibb stared at the kite for a long time and remembered an afternoon that suddenly felt as distant as the moon, when he had been almost like a child again himself, as he played with the boy who could have been his son.

No doubt whoever had taken Beep thought Gibb was his father and believed they could hold him up because of it. That—not his relationship to Ben Armentrout—was the reason the child had been kidnapped, of course. Lindsay hadn't quite said so, but it was plain from what she'd said about the plant that she knew it.

But if most of Elmwood knew the truth about Beep, perhaps that would help to target the search. Who *didn't* know that Beep wasn't his? Who had reason to believe that Gibb held a special affection for that child?

Nearly everybody, he concluded. Half the town must have walked by Lindsay's courtyard that afternoon when they had washed the Lincoln. And the other half had no doubt watched them flying the kite in the courthouse square the week before. So that line of reasoning got him precisely nowhere.

Gibb swore under his breath. Why had he even come here to Beep's room? he wondered. There would be no clues in the apartment, and probably none in the building. If there was anything to be found, it would be outside, where Beep had been snatched. Somewhere between the back door and the drugstore, there must be some hint of what had happened.

He turned on his heel to go downstairs to look, and his gaze fell on a framed sampler hanging above the desk. Beep's name and his birth statistics—weight, length, date—were neatly embroidered in the center of a linen square, surrounded by a border of alphabet blocks. Gibb's eyes skimmed carelessly over the information and focused on the date.

And he realized that the house of cards he'd been building in his mind all this time was slowly collapsing, and that nothing could stop its fall.

Lindsay had lied to him. Her son hadn't celebrated his eighth birthday in the last couple of months, as she'd implied. Beep was closer to nine. Which meant he wasn't the child of a careless affair a few months after her divorce; he'd been born a bare eight months after that final, horrible quarrel between Gibb and Lindsay.

Between *his parents*—for now Gibb knew that Lindsay's son was his, as well.

Lindsay was sitting in the kitchen, on a straight chair drawn up by the window, her spine rigidly upright, when Gibb came back. "Wouldn't you be more comfortable in a different chair?" he asked.

The words were mild, but she could hear tension in his voice, and it comforted her a little to know that Beep's danger was weighing heavily on Gibb, as well. She shook her head. "I'm all right. I can see from here." She knew he was studying her, but she didn't shift her gaze from the courtyard below. "And I don't particularly want to be comfortable just now, when Beep might be in pain."

"Stop it, Lindsay. You'll drive yourself crazy." His tone was harsh, and he paused before saying, more gently, "The chief hasn't come?"

"Not yet."

"Well, he had a bunch of things to set in motion. And he said he'd have to be a bit careful when he comes, so he doesn't rouse suspicion if someone's watching."

The idea that someone might be posted nearby, keeping an eye on the building, made Lindsay shiver.

Gibb swore under his breath. "I'm sorry. I shouldn't have said it that way."

Lindsay licked her lips. "It's all right. It's different for you."

"Oh, it is?" His voice held an edge like a steel sword.

Lindsay turned to stare at him. Then she caught movement from the corner of her eye and swung around to watch as a car pulled up by the courtyard. It was not one of Elmwood's marked patrol cars, but the chief's private vehicle.

"This is a bad idea," Lindsay said suddenly. "Everybody in Elmwood knows him. If they're watching—"

"What do you suggest?" Gibb's voice was dry. "Shall we just sit here and wait for further orders, like obedient children?"

"I don't know."

"Probably nobody's watching, anyway. That 'no cops' line is pretty standard fare—anybody who's ever watched television knows that much. Besides, there can't be too many people involved in this conspiracy, or surely somebody would have had enough sense to call a halt to it."

Lindsay suspected there was something wrong with his reasoning, but she appreciated the effort to comfort her, nonetheless. She decided she must have been imagining the sharpness in his voice a few moments before.

The chief leaned into the back of his car and picked up an enormous potted plant. Without hurry, he crossed the courtyard, pausing to admire the fountain despite its winter wrappings. A moment later Lindsay heard his footsteps on the staircase.

He came in and set the plant on the table.

"What's that?" Lindsay asked.

"That's the potted yucca my wife promised you. Or, rather, that I'm pretending she promised you. The story is I said I'd drop it off on my way to have coffee with the guys. Awful of her to make me run errands on my Sunday off." Despite the teasing quality of the words, his tone was dead serious. "I'm sorry it took me a while to get here. A crew from the state evidence lab is on the way, and I've put out an alert and a call for all the officers I can get. Did you say there's a note?"

Gibb pointed at the paper, still lying on the kitchen table. "It's been touched pretty much all over, I'm afraid."

"Well, we don't see too many of these in a town this size," the chief said, and pulled a pair of tongs from his pocket. "I can understand why everybody'd forget about fingerprints. But maybe we can still isolate some recognizable ones. And we should be able to figure out pretty quickly which newspapers and magazines the headlines came from." He slid the note into a clear plastic bag before he read the message. Then he looked thoughtfully from Lindsay to Gibb. "How long have you two been divorced?"

"What's that got to do with anything?" Lindsay asked.

"Nine years," Gibb said.

"Had any custody battles?"

Lindsay said tightly, "Of course not. And Gibb would have no reason to take Beep, so if that's what you're implying—"

"Or maybe I'm thinking that you did," the chief said pleasantly. "It's not very likely, I'd say, but the family situation is a factor we always have to consider—especially when there are divorced parents involved."

Lindsay was furious, and frantic. Was that why Gibb had searched the building—because he thought she might have hidden her own son? "That's absolutely insane! Now can we stop playing stupid games and do something to find my child?"

"Come on, Lindsay." Gibb put a hand on her shoulder. "There have been no custody battles, Chief. And both Lindsay and I are well accounted for all afternoon. I suppose either of us could have an accomplice, but I fail to see what we'd have to gain by kidnapping the child.''

The chief made no comment, but his bright, slightly beady eyes studied them both for a long moment. "Any idea who might have it in for either of you?"

"I can give you a few names at the plant," Gibb said.

"Good—make a list. We'll start a search in the neighborhood as soon as I have the manpower. I'm afraid it will have to be pretty quiet, to avoid arousing any more suspicion than necessary." He added thoughtfully, "Perhaps we'll announce that one of our illustrious citizens has reported a missing wallet."

"We understand," Gibb said.

"As soon as you get that list together, I'll start checking up on everyone—find out where they've been today. What was the child wearing, Lindsay?"

She closed her eyes and tried to picture Beep as she had seen him last. "Blue jeans and a black sweatshirt with his school mascot on the front. I've got a recent photo, if that would help."

The chief nodded. "It sure would. Any idea why the note's addressed to you, Gibb?"

"Obviously someone thinks I'll pay—one way or another—to get my son back."

Lindsay's knees buckled, and only the iron grip of Gibb's hand on her arm kept her from falling. The chief put her into her chair and tried to push her head between her knees, but she struggled. "I'm not going to faint," she argued. "And I have to get that photograph."

They let her go, then. She found a couple of snapshots and Beep's last school picture.

Not his *last*, she told herself with a gasp. His *latest*. Beep's whole life lay before him; she wouldn't let it be any other way.

The chief took the photographs and the note and went away.

Gibb was standing by the kitchen window, staring down at the courtyard, apparently oblivious to Lindsay's presence. She watched him for a moment, then started to tiptoe out of the room.

He didn't turn, but his voice, soft and level, reached out to snare her like a fisherman's hook. "According to the sampler on Benjamin's wall, he was born eight months after I left."

Lindsay shrugged. "Just ask the town gossips. They'll tell you I was having an affair and that's why I wanted to split up my marriage."

"No. Afterward, maybe—but you weren't messing around behind my back. I'd have known." His voice was utterly flat, as if he was stating a fact that was obvious but insignificant. "Why did you lie to me, Lindsay? Why did you tell me that he wasn't mine?"

She hesitated, then told the truth. "Because you didn't want him. You never wanted him."

He turned to face her, squaring his shoulders as if he was assuming a burden. "That's right—I didn't. And I made myself very clear. But you didn't believe me, did you? You deliberately went against my wishes and created a child you knew very well I didn't want."

"Lots of people think they don't like kids, Gibb, and then they find that having their own is different. I thought you'd change your mind."

"So without even discussing it with me—"

"You *wouldn't* discuss it!"

"We had an agreement to use the pill, Lindsay—but despite that, you intentionally set out to have a child."

She made a hopeless little gesture. "It wasn't anywhere near as calculated as you make it sound."

"Then what do you call it?"

"Does it matter any more? It's a long time ago. Beep's part of this world now, whether you wanted him to be or not—and he's in danger. That's the only thing I care about."

The back door banged, and Ben Armentrout took the steps three at a time. "Lindsay!" he shouted, at the top. "Oh, sweetheart—"

"You may not be able to fix this one, Ben," Gibb said quietly, and walked away.

None of them talked much after that. Heidi went home. Ben sat at the kitchen table, his head in his hands. Gibb had moved to the living room window and stood staring across the courthouse square. Lindsay hovered beside the silent telephone.

Somewhere along the line she had put down Beep's stuffed elephant and picked up Spats instead. The warm weight of the cat in her arms was a tiny bit of comfort, and his raspy purr seemed to say that everything would be all right.

Ben pushed his chair back from the table and made a pot of coffee, and when it had finished dripping Lindsay went into the living room to ask Gibb if he wanted a cup.

He didn't say a word, just shook his head. He was staring at the courthouse tower, Lindsay realized, and her heart twisted a little in sympathy for the pain he must be feeling. In a way, she supposed, his torment might be even greater than her own—for he had lost a son he didn't know he'd possessed.

"You didn't just build a kite that day," she said softly. "You were building memories."

She thought he hadn't heard, but finally he shook his head a little. "You don't begin to understand, Lindsay."

He sounded tired, she thought, not angry anymore. "I wish you'd tell me," she said carefully.

He shook his head.

Though she stood there for another minute, he still hadn't looked at her. "I was wrong, Gibb," she said. "I was thinking only of myself. I had my husband, my honeymoon home, my life all arranged the way I wanted it. The one thing that was missing was a child."

"A child I didn't want." His voice was uncompromising.

Lindsay whispered, "I thought you were being selfish, not to let me have what I wanted so badly. And I thought I knew best."

He didn't answer.

"But I'm not sorry," she went on firmly. "For the last eight years, I've had a wonderful little boy to share my life. What have you had, Gibb?"

She walked away, and paused at the top of the stairs. "I'm going out to join the search," she said, without looking at either Gibb or Ben. "I want to be there when they find him."

She'd forgotten about the cat; she was still carrying him as she went down the stairs. She'd almost reached the bottom when Gibb leaned over the top of the rail and said, "Lindsay, wait. I'll go with you."

She didn't look at him. "You don't need to."

"Your father can stay by the phone. Lindsay—honey…."

She stopped then, and looked up at him.

Gibb came slowly down the stairs. "I'm sorry for so many things," he whispered, and put his arms around her.

She released a little whimpering sigh and put her head on his shoulder. It felt good to be sheltered once more by the warmth of his body; without thinking, she turned her face up to his. "Oh, Gibb—"

His kiss was soft, gentle, tender—and as Lindsay responded, he drew her slowly closer, till she felt as if her body was melting into his.

Spats objected violently to being squeezed; he yowled and wriggled till Lindsay stepped back and put him down, and he shot down the remaining few stairs into the storeroom.

Gibb slid an arm around Lindsay's shoulders. "Let's go look for our son."

There was a tiny rustle among the empty boxes piled under the stairs, and in the center of the storeroom Spats froze in his classic hunter's pose, tail straight out, body hunched, staring toward the noise.

"Is he after a mouse?" Gibb said.

"I suppose so. I've never had one before, though."

The rustle grew, and a stack of boxes tipped over and scattered across the storeroom floor.

"That's one hell of a mouse," Gibb said. He took the last few stairs with a leap and started tugging at stacks of boxes, and then at something else—the sleeve of a black sweatshirt.

Lindsay's heart caught in her throat.

Beep stood up and shook himself and grinned. "I was coming out," he said. "You didn't need to drag me. I was getting pretty tired of being in there anyway. I'd read all my comic books, and my soda wasn't cold any more. And I forgot to bring a sandwich, so I was getting hungry, too."

Lindsay sat down on the stairs as if her knees had evaporated. "You did this *yourself*?" she gasped.

Beep nodded. "Did the note scare you? I thought it was pretty good. I got the idea from a movie I saw a while back. There was this really neat kidnapping, see, and—"

"But why?" she whispered.

Beep shrugged. "I thought if you guys had to stop arguing so much, you might decide you liked each other, after all. And I was right, wasn't I, 'cause you do. I saw that mushy kiss." He turned to look at Gibb. "Hey, did you mean it? Are you *really* my dad?"

CHAPTER TEN

GIBB'S voice sounded like the crack of a bullwhip. "How *dare* you scare your mother to death like this, Benjamin?"

Beep stared at him. All the color drained out of the child's face as the enormity of his deed began to sink in. "I guess... I..."

Lindsay managed to stand up, but she had to clutch the stair rail for support. "Gibb—"

Gibb ignored her. "There is no excuse for this!" He turned on his heel and yanked the back door open. "I'm going out to find the police chief and the people who are looking for you, Benjamin—and you will apologize to each and every one of them, if it takes all night."

Beep gulped. "Yes, sir," he whispered.

The door slammed. Lindsay sank down on the step again and stared at her son, who was standing like a statue in the center of the storeroom, looking woebegone. She didn't know whether to hug him or paddle him. She settled for a talking-to instead. "Benjamin Patrick Gardner, you have never seen trouble like you're in now. Isn't it bad enough that you were already grounded for misbehaving? How could you pull a stunt like this?"

"I didn't break the rules," Beep said. His voice was a little quavery. "You said I couldn't leave the building, and I didn't. I only told Heidi I was going to. That's not the same thing at all."

Ben looked down the stairs. "Did I hear—Beep!" He almost ran down the stairs and swept the child into his arms. "You're not hurt? Oh, my darling boy, everything's all right now."

"No, it's not, Daddy. By now, your darling boy is the subject of a nationwide alert," Lindsay said dryly. "He'll probably be a whimpering puddle by the time the police chief gets finished scolding him. Then I'm going to lock him in his room on bread and water till he's grown a beard, and—"

Beep's face crumpled. "But I just wanted..." He gave one small pitiful sob, broke away from Ben and rushed into Lindsay's arms. Suddenly he was a tiny child again, crying out his pain, needing his mother's comfort. "Is he really my dad?"

"Yes, my dear." She stroked his hair and nestled him close, as she had thought she might never be able to do again, and closed her eyes in gratitude.

She was still holding him when Gibb came back.

He looked sternly at the child. "Huddling in your mother's arms is not going to get you out of this, Benjamin."

Beep shivered and hid his face deeper in Lindsay's shoulder. Her arms tightened around him.

Gibb frowned at her. "Lindsay, I'm not going to argue with you." His voice was quiet but firm. "The chief has called in all the searchers, and I'm determined that Benjamin's going to face up to his responsibility and apologize."

"Who's arguing?" she said mildly. "I think it's a dandy idea." She urged Beep to his feet. "But I'll come with him, if you don't mind."

The courtyard was full of men and women. Some were friends and neighbors. But the majority Lindsay had never seen before. Many were in uniform. She was surprised at how many people there were; the search might have been a quiet one, as the chief had put it, but it certainly hadn't been small.

Beep's eyes widened in shock. "All these people were looking for *me*?" he whispered.

"Just for you, pal," Gibb said. "You created a whole lot bigger stir than you bargained for, and ruined a Sunday afternoon for a whole lot of nice people. So what do you have to say to them now?"

Beep clung to Lindsay's arm, trying to hide his face in her sleeve, till Gibb took his elbow and gently led him out to the center of the courtyard. He stood beside the child, one hand on his shoulder, as Beep stumbled through a tearful apology.

Lindsay thought her heart would overflow at the sight of the tall man and the little boy, standing together and facing the world in partnership. That had always been her dream, she admitted, even in the years when she had thought she would never see Gibb again, and that he would never know his son.

They moved slowly among the crowd, Gibb's hand still resting on Beep's shoulder as the child faced and thanked each person who had helped in the investigation. Lindsay was shaking from the strain by the time it was over and the crowd had slowly dispersed.

The police chief was the last to leave. "See?" he told Lindsay with a wry smile as he put the potted yucca in his car. "Like I said, in cases like this you always have to consider the family!"

The silence in the courtyard was deafening. Ben looked from Gibb's set face to Lindsay's, and said, "Well, I guess you have some things to talk about, and I'd only be in the way. Shall I take Beep with me?"

"And reward him with toys or ice cream?" Lindsay shook her head. "No, Daddy."

"Well, I wasn't intending to reward him, exactly. I was just so glad to have him safe..." Ben's voice trailed off. "I see what you mean. I'll be going, then."

Beep's feet dragged as the three of them climbed the stairs to the apartment. The moment they reached the kitchen, Gibb said, "I think perhaps you should go to your room, Benjamin. I imagine your mother still has a few things to say to you—but I need to talk to her for a minute right now."

"Yes, sir." Beep shuffled off toward his room, head drooping.

As soon as the child was out of sight, Gibb said, "I'm sorry if you feel that I butted in. I didn't stop to think about that till it was all over."

"Not at all. I think you handled it very well."

"It just seemed the obvious thing to do, to make sure he realized the trouble he'd caused."

"It wouldn't have been obvious to everyone." She was thinking of Ben, and she suspected Gibb was, too. "I think you're a natural parent, as a matter of fact—"

He held up a hand. "Dammit, Lindsay, stop trying to manipulate me!"

Lindsay had never before heard such sharpness in his voice. "I'm not," she protested. "I meant it as a compliment."

Gibb took a deep breath. "Look, I'm glad you have your son back."

"*My* son? When he was still missing, you were talking about *our* son. You were actually acting like a father—"

"I came to my senses, all right? Nothing's really changed, you know, so stop pretending that it has."

Lindsay felt angry color rising in her face. "Don't patronize me, Gibb!"

He didn't seem to hear. "I'll make whatever arrangements are necessary for financial support."

"I don't want your money!"

"You may need it, if I can't pull your father's plant out of this slump."

Lindsay couldn't exactly argue with that, but pride kept her from admitting it. "I'd rather starve," she snapped.

"Don't be a fool. My lawyer will be in touch about the details."

Gibb's hand was already on the newel post at the top of the stairs when Lindsay said, "Don't you think we should work out things like visits, instead of leaving it to lawyers?"

Gibb shook his head. "There's no need to worry about that. All I agreed to was financial support, Lindsay."

She was stunned. "Don't you even want to see him?"

"The way I live would make visits very difficult."

"That's no answer!"

He turned to face her. "Do you want me to spell it out, Lindsay? I told you before, nothing has changed. I'll pay for his needs, because that's my responsibility. But that's a long way from wanting every other weekend and a month in the summer."

Lindsay was silent. Gibb was right about the difficulties. The work schedule he kept and the way he moved around from job to job would make any sort of regular visitation a nightmare. But to say that he didn't want to see Beep at all—

"He's your son, too," she said finally.

"Must I remind you? That was your choice, not mine."

He moved quietly down the stairs and out of sight, but Lindsay knew the precise moment when the door closed behind him. She knew, as well, that he wouldn't be coming back, and all the hope she had so recently rediscovered drained once more from her life.

The second disillusionment was worse, she realized. Nine years ago, she'd had the resilience of youth on her side. Now she felt old, tired, worn out.

She'd been right all those years ago, when she had chosen to bar him from her life rather than tell him that he'd fathered her child. She had done what she needed to do; she had protected herself and her son.

But it was no comfort now to know that she had made the correct choice. For only now did she realize that her decision not to inform Gibb about the baby had risen not only from self-protection, but from denial. So long as she didn't tell him, she could pretend in the deepest corners of her heart that if he had known, he would not have turned his back on her—on *them*—after all.

She had nursed that fantasy, and kept it so dark that even she hadn't been completely aware of its existence, for nine long years. And as she had watched Gibb over the past couple of weeks while he got acquainted with his son, that hidden fantasy had rooted deeper and sent out new green shoots of hope and wonder about the family they could have been...the family she still wanted them to be.

But now she had to face a double-barreled blow, the shattering of fantasies both old and new. Gibb knew the truth, and still he had cold-bloodedly walked away. He didn't care enough for either Lindsay or Beep to let them have even the smallest place in his life.

She could accept that verdict for herself. The hurts of nine years ago had run deep, and though she had worked through her pain to a realization of the love that still lay buried beneath, she could understand why Gibb might not have been able to reach the same result. But she could not forgive the slight to his son. Beep had never done anything to hurt him.

And it would be Beep whose heart would ache the hardest.

Days went by without a sight of Gibb. The bounce in Beep's step seemed to have been permanently dispelled. Even more worrisome, in Lindsay's opinion, was the way he immediately and carefully followed orders and carried out requests.

The night he cleared the dinner table without being asked, Lindsay took his temperature. She was almost disappointed when the thermometer reading was normal, for she could do something about a fever. She didn't know how to nurse a heartbreak.

He was still grounded, of course, which didn't help the moodiness level for either of them. Sometimes, Lindsay thought, grounding a child was more punishment for the parent than for the kid.

She sprinkled spices over the top of three salmon steaks and slid the pan under the broiler. "Beep—time to set the table. Your grandpa will be here in a few minutes."

Beep put down his book and came obediently to the kitchen. "What's for dinner?"

"Salmon and wild rice."

He didn't make the gagging noise with which he often greeted the news of fish on the menu. He just got plates from the cabinet. "Why hasn't Gibb... Why hasn't Dad come to see me?"

"I don't know, dear. I haven't seen him, either."

"Is he still mad at me about the kidnapping thing?"

"I don't think he ever was, really. He was worried and disappointed, as I was."

Beep sighed. "I guess I really blew it, huh?"

She was saved from having to answer by Ben, who came up the stairs with a hearty greeting and a brown paper bag under his arm.

Lindsay eyed it warily. "Daddy, if you've brought another present for Beep because you're sorry that he's confined to the apartment—"

"No, dear." Ben pulled out two bottles—one champagne, one sparkling grape juice. He flourished the champagne and said, "I'm declaring this a celebration. So wipe the glumness off those faces, you two, and let's have a party."

Lindsay handed him a pair of champagne flutes and said practically, "What are we celebrating?"

Ben didn't answer till he'd popped the cork and filled her glass. "The new incarnation of Armentrout Industries." He poured grape juice for Beep and clicked his glass against the child's. "We signed a contract today to produce a new sort of battery. It's a brand-new technology, and we'll be the first to have it on the market— a higher-powered battery with a longer-lasting charge, which will give electric cars a much greater range and make them a practical alternative to the gasoline engine within a couple of years."

Lindsay stared at him. "So Gibb pulled it off," she whispered.

"He did, indeed." Ben took Lindsay's untouched glass and set it aside, slid an arm around her waist and waltzed her around the kitchen. "Which means, my pretty, that in the long run, dividends will go up, the Armentrout Trust will have money to burn—"

And Gibb would leave, Lindsay thought. Once she had wished for that day. Now she didn't know what to think. It might be easier, knowing he was gone. And yet there was an empty hole in her heart at the idea of never catching a glimpse of him again.

And what about Beep?

He was showing the first enthusiasm she'd seen all week, as he begged Ben for a full explanation of the new technology. Lindsay only half listened as she stirred the pot of wild rice. Obviously Beep hadn't yet reasoned beyond Gibb's success. And when he did...

"You're not drinking that champagne, my girl," Ben accused.

"I'm happy for you, Daddy."

Ben watched her for a long moment. "I was hoping you and Gibb would patch it up, Lindsay."

She shrugged. "It takes two."

"Gibb's a good man."

Lindsay tried to smile. "I guess he's more than paid back that settlement you gave him nine years ago."

"Oh, he did that long since." He paused to sip his champagne. "Not long after Triangle got off the ground, in fact—though of course at the time I had no idea where he got the money."

She stared at him. "You never said anything about that before!"

"Gibb didn't want me to tell you. And it wasn't as if I knew anything, anyway—I just got a check in the mail and a note saying he'd appreciate it if I respected his privacy." Ben shrugged. "So I did."

Beep polished off his grape juice and reached for the bottle. "If my dad won't be so busy at the plant," he said, almost to himself, "maybe now he'll have time for me."

Lindsay bit her lip. She hadn't told Beep that Gibb had no intention of seeing him again. The truth had looked too savage, and Beep had been too fragile that night after the kidnapping when they had talked. So she had kept her own counsel.

Now she regretted it. However harsh the truth, it would have been better to get it over with, rather than to feed impossible dreams.

Ben was watching her intently. "Lindsay—"

"Beep, go wash up," she interrupted. "The salmon's almost ready."

He made a disapproving face. "Fish," he said, under his breath.

The moment he was out of earshot, Ben asked, "Hasn't Gibb even seen him since the kidnapping?"

Lindsay shook her head.

Ben sighed. "I thought . . . There's something else you should know, honey. I've offered Gibb a majority interest in the plant."

"Oh, Daddy—" She had believed that she would never feel hope again, but there seemed to be a balloon inside her chest slowly inflating with a substance that made her feel lighter than air. If Gibb owned a good share of the plant, he wouldn't go away forever. He'd have to come back now and then. Or he might even stay.

"Why shouldn't I?" Ben said gruffly. "Without him, there wouldn't be anything left at all. It was his connections that got the new contract, so I thought he should have the chance to stick around and capitalize on what he'd started." He raised his glass and studied the bubbles rising in the clear wine. "He turned it down, Lindsay. In fact, he's leaving tomorrow. But I thought he'd see Beep, at least, before he went."

Lindsay's balloon burst. Every nerve in her body seemed to be humming, all at different pitches and frequencies that formed a cacophony, which echoed through her aching head.

Beep bounded into the kitchen and stopped whistling to ask, "Mom, does my dad like—"

"Not now, Beep." Her voice was sharp.

Beep stared at her in dismay, then burst into tears. "You said you'd never get angry with me for asking about my dad!"

Lindsay put a hand to her temple. "I'm sorry, darling. Yes, I did say that. And I'm not angry. It's just not a good time—"

"But you said!" He was almost wailing. "All I did was ask, and you yelled at me! My dad hates me and my mom—"

Lindsay had had as much as she could take. "Beep, for heaven's sake, nobody hates you!"

"But he hasn't even come to see me. He must hate me! *Everybody* hates me!" He stamped off to his room, and the door slammed so hard the building seemed to reverberate.

Lindsay counted to ten, and then to twenty, and decided to let Beep cool off for a while. "Well, Daddy— would you like to try the salmon?"

"Some celebration, huh?" Ben said.

Lindsay managed three bites before she pushed her plate aside and went to Beep's room. The lights were off, and he was lying on his stomach across the bed. "Honey?" she whispered.

He wouldn't look at her, but he didn't move away as she sat down beside him and smoothed his hair.

"I'm sorry you don't have your dad, Beep. Sometimes these things just don't work out."

"Why?" It was only a breath, but the single word carried a million questions, and Lindsay's heart felt the weight of them all.

"I don't know the answer to that, sweetheart. But we still have each other, and we always will."

She thought for a while he hadn't heard her, but finally he sniffed and sat up and put his head on her shoulder. Silent tears soaked the soft cotton of her blouse. After a while, he dozed off, and she settled him carefully against his pillow and went out to the living room.

Ben was still sitting at the kitchen table, picking at his dinner. "Is he all right?"

"I suppose so. Daddy, will you stay a while? There's something I have to do."

He nodded, and before she could lose her nerve Lindsay grabbed up the nearest sweater and hurried downstairs, through the store and across the square to the Olivers' apartment.

She rang the doorbell twice, and she'd almost given up when Gibb answered. A stack of folded shirts was cradled in his arms, and he looked warily at her.

Lindsay licked her lips. "Daddy said you were leaving tomorrow."

"That's right. So whatever this is about, I honestly don't have time, Lindsay."

"It won't take long. I'm sorry to annoy you, but you did promise me a donation for the crisis center, and they really need the money."

For a moment she thought he was going to shut the door in her face. "I'd forgotten. Sorry. Come in and I'll write a check."

She followed him across the living room. On the table by the window, a briefcase stood open, neatly packed with his laptop computer and office supplies. A suitcase stood by the couch, packed and ready to take out to the car. He set the stack of shirts on a chair and dug a checkbook from a pocket of the briefcase.

"I understand the plant has a new contract," Lindsay said.

"Yes."

"Daddy seems very pleased."

"If Ben plays his cards right, he'll be smack in the middle of a tub of honey. He'll already be manufacturing, while everybody else is still thinking about it. And if all goes well, you won't have to solicit donations for the trust any more." He waved the check in the air to dry the ink, then handed it to her and put his fountain pen in his shirt pocket.

"He told me."

"If that's all—"

"It isn't." She steeled herself. "Beep misses you, Gibb. He cried himself to sleep just now because he wants to have a relationship with you."

"I'm sorry, but I can't do that."

Fury seemed to burn a hole straight through Lindsay's brain. "Why? He absolutely adores you—God knows why! And you seemed to like him well enough, too, till you found out he was yours! Why won't you even give him a chance?"

"I told you—I can't, Lindsay."

He sounded almost tormented, she thought. "Can't?" she said slowly. She dug her fists into her hips and looked at him. "I am not leaving till you explain that."

"I could throw you out."

"Try it." He didn't answer, and after a moment she spoke again, more gently. "Gibb, I have to tell him *something*. If there's a reason, please tell me. Right now he thinks you hate him."

Gibb swore.

But Lindsay's instincts said something had changed. She could feel a difference in him—something gentler, more approachable—and she almost held her breath as she waited.

He sighed. "What's the first thing you remember?"

Lindsay was puzzled. "About you?"

"No. The earliest memory you have from childhood."

She considered. "My mother, coming in to kiss me good-night before she went to a party. It must have been a costume ball, or perhaps I only thought she looked like a princess. Why?"

"The first memory I have is a beating." There was a raspy edge to his voice, as if he had to force the words out. "I don't recall what I'd done—if it was anything at all. I just remember the belt hitting me, and trying to get away from it. But I couldn't. I was three, I think."

Lindsay closed her eyes, but she couldn't shut out the pain in his voice or the picture in her mind. "Oh, Gibb..."

"I'm sure that wasn't the first time, just the earliest I recall. And it certainly wasn't the last."

He was looking at her, but Lindsay was positive he didn't see her. He was staring inward, at a private kind of hell. In broken sentences, as if the words were being dragged from him, he told her of his childhood—the beatings he had taken, and the ones he'd watched his mother suffer from the men who had come and gone in her life. Bruises, black eyes, broken bones...the catalog went on and on.

Lindsay wanted to touch him, to hold him, to comfort him—but she knew that just now there was no way to reach him. All she could do was wait for the pain to spill out and hope that once he had drained the wound, there would be a chance to heal.

It was almost half an hour before he stopped talking, and even then, when she reached out to touch him gently, he moved away. "I don't know why I told you all that. I've never told anyone before."

"Perhaps you needed to get rid of it," Lindsay said softly.

"Don't tell Beep the details, all right? There's no need to upset him with all of it. But at least you know why I can't take the chance. Maybe someday he'll understand that it isn't him—this is my fault."

Lindsay frowned. "You won't see Beep because you were abused," she said slowly. "Because you're afraid you'll abuse him."

Gibb nodded. "I'm afraid of being alone with him— or any child—for more than a few minutes. I'm afraid of the anger that's inside me. You work with the crisis shelter, Lindsay. You know that boys who are battered grow up to be men who are batterers."

"Not all of them."

"Too many. Are you willing to risk Beep on that percentage?"

She understood what he was saying. She knew the statistics weren't pretty.

"I took that chance once, with you," Gibb said quietly. "I made a bet with fate that I could keep my anger under control."

"And you did."

"But that's not the point. I shouldn't have put you at risk, and I won't take the chance again—especially not with a child."

The hard, uncompromising note was in his voice, and it made Lindsay furious. "So you'd orphan your son instead?'' She squared her shoulders. ''You know something, Gibb? You're a coward.''

''You're entitled to think as you like.''

''You fathered this child, but you're too chicken to even try to be a daddy!''

''If you'd only believed me when I said I didn't want kids—''

''I know you'd rather he hadn't been born. But what am I supposed to do now? Take him out and shoot him?''

''Lindsay, stop it. Don't you see this is tearing me up?''

She didn't stop; she couldn't. ''You were a failure as a husband—and Beep's lucky you don't want to have anything to do with him. Do you hear me? *Lucky*!''

The word seemed to bounce around the room, echoing from wall to wall and slowly dying into silence.

''You're right.'' Gibb sounded exhausted. ''That's exactly what I've been trying to tell you. Now would you please go?''

''No.'' Lindsay was trembling, now that it was too late to back down from the risk she had taken. She had staked everything on this chance, and her life—her child's life—hung in the balance. ''Don't you see, Gibb? You just proved the only thing you need to. If the string of insults I just flung at you wasn't enough to make you want to hit me, nothing would. But you didn't do it. You didn't even consider it—did you?''

''No. But...'' He stared at her. ''What do you think you're doing, Lindsay?''

''When Beep pulled off that damnable kidnapping stunt, you must have wanted to paddle him within an inch of his life. I certainly did—if ever a child deserved a good tanning, it was him. But instead you made him face up to what he'd done. You didn't punish him—you disciplined him, guided him. You touched him in love, not anger." She was crying; she felt like a baby blubbering foolishly, but she had to say it fast or it would never be said. "It takes a whole lot more courage to be gentle than to be a bully. Don't you know yourself better than that?"

"You made that scene just now on purpose?"

"I know more about you than you do. I always have! I was so sure that you'd love a baby—our baby. I saw something in you that you still don't see—a gentleness that would make you a wonderful father. I was so certain of it I was willing to take the risk that you'd be furious with me for a while, because I was convinced in the end, once our baby was in your arms..."

He was standing like a stone. Perhaps, she thought, he was seeing himself for the first time as he really was.

"I wanted your child, Gibb, and I was terrified that you'd decide the pill wasn't certain enough and you'd do something permanent. So I managed to convince myself that what I was doing was noble, not underhanded and sneaky—and I stopped taking the pill."

He shook his head.

Lindsay said quietly, "I was going to tell you I was pregnant, the day we had that last awful quarrel. I'd just found out myself, you see, that very morning, with one of those home-testing kits. It wasn't very smart, I know—but I was pretty scared to face you, so I went shopping, to make myself feel better. And when I saw the perfect set of nursery furniture, I bought the whole thing. I guess I thought it would make you feel better, too. Make the baby more real, somehow."

"You never told me what you'd bought," Gibb said. "Just that you'd spent a fortune on furniture."

She smiled ruefully. "Not very well phrased, was it? But how could I tell you then, when you were already angry? I tried to hint about having a baby someday, and you—"

Gibb rubbed the back of his neck as if it hurt. "I told you in no uncertain terms that there would never be one, didn't I? And I wouldn't listen."

"I'm the one who should have listened. I should have believed you and asked why you didn't want a child. I guess I was afraid I couldn't convince you with logic, so I was scared to try." She stopped and went on even more softly, "And I think I knew even then that you weren't willing to share your whole self, Gibb, and that meant you could leave me at any time. So I wanted a part of you that would be mine to keep—always mine."

Gibb was silent for a long moment. "He's a very special kid, Lindsay. He's what I could have been, if I'd had some love along the way."

"It's not too late. He wants to love you, Gibb."

"I intended never to get close to any kid. But Beep's the kind who won't let you keep your distance, isn't he? I've had to admit that this week. Staying away has been the toughest thing I've ever done." He smiled wistfully. "He's like you, Lindsay. You wouldn't let me stay away, either. I never intended to fall in love with you—either time."

She wasn't sure she was hearing properly. "*Either* time?"

"All those years ago. And just a few weeks back, when I saw you again." He brushed a wisp of hair from her forehead; Lindsay saw with astonishment that his fingers were trembling. "I failed you so badly, my darling— nine years ago, and again this week when I tried to turn my back and pretend nothing had changed. I don't deserve anything, Lindsay. Certainly not a second chance."

She tried to speak, but her throat was so tight she couldn't make a sound.

"You said Beep wanted to love me. What about you, Lindsay? Is there any chance at all that you—"

She never knew what she said. Perhaps it wasn't words at all—but it didn't matter, for a moment later she was in his arms, and all the passion she had hidden deep within her for so long exploded with the power of his kiss.

Finally he buried his face in her hair and whispered, "I love you more than life, Lindsay. I always have. I was stunned, you know, when I actually married you, because I never intended to let myself get so close to anyone. But you..."

She remembered that bewildered look at the church altar, and how it had confused her. "I knew a good thing when I saw it," she said huskily. "And I still do."

"Are you sure? I love you both too much to risk your safety."

Lindsay smiled at him with all the love and reassurance she possessed. "I'm sure."

He looked deep into her eyes for a long moment and said huskily, "Then I guess I'll have to ask Ben if his offer is still good."

Lindsay was almost breathless with happiness. "Does that mean you'd stay here to run the plant?"

"Ben told you about it? I'd like to sell my share of Triangle and settle down. In fact, I've been a little irritable ever since Ben made me that offer, because it sounded so good and I knew I couldn't accept it, the way things were. But now—" His arms tightened around her.

Lindsay smiled. "Now," she said softly, "it's time to go home to our son."

EPILOGUE

BEEP'S throaty chuckle woke Lindsay on the morning of her birthday shortly after the sun came up. Mingled with the deeper tones of his father's voice, it formed a sonata so beautiful it clutched at Lindsay's heart and brought a misty smile to her lips.

Her husband, her son, a brilliant new day for all of them to explore—what more could any woman ask for a birthday gift?

She was just sliding her feet into her fuzzy slippers when the bedroom door opened. "Mom!" Beep dragged the word out into multiple syllables. "You're not supposed to be up. We made you breakfast in bed!"

Behind him, Gibb was carrying a tray. His gaze met hers, and he smiled—and Lindsay felt a soft, familiar dizziness at the very corners of her mind. She hoped she never stopped feeling that way when he smiled at her.

Obediently, she got back into bed. Gibb arranged the tray on her lap and sat down on the edge of the mattress; Beep climbed up beside her and plopped down with his legs folded under him, nearly upsetting her breakfast.

Lindsay surveyed the tray. Hot toasted bagels, cream cheese, jam, orange juice, coffee... and on a small plate in the middle, a familiar-looking square red velvet box.

"That's your birthday present," Beep said cheerfully. "I earned the money for it myself. A lot of it, at least, but Dad helped, so it's kinda from both of us."

There was always a faint undertone in Beep's voice when he said "Dad," Lindsay had noticed, as if he, too, still couldn't quite believe his good fortune.

She picked up the box and looked at Gibb. "You were buying it for Beep?" she said softly.

It was Beep who answered. "Of course. Remember? I couldn't go to the store, 'cause I didn't get ungrounded till the wedding. So I asked Dad to do it."

So that was why Gibb had been at Henderson's Jewelry and why he'd so smoothly hidden his purchase from her. And it explained the conversation she'd overheard a few days before that, too—when Beep had asked a favor and Gibb had protested.

She smiled softly at both of them and opened the box.

Suspended from a dainty gold chain was a delicate filigree ornament, barely an inch across, which spelled out *I LOVE YOU*. The *O* in *love* had been replaced, however, with a diamond at least a quarter of a carat in size.

That part must have been Dad's contribution, Lindsay thought with a tinge of humor. She was so touched that she couldn't even speak—not by the diamond, but by the image of Gibb buying that trinket for Beep's sake, and then adding his own expression of love.

She wasn't capable of voicing her feelings just then, so she reached for Gibb instead. The breakfast tray rocked, but Lindsay didn't notice. He kissed her long and deeply, and she was utterly breathless by the time he raised his head.

"Geez," Beep said, and sat back on his heels. "If you guys are going to get mushy again, can I at least eat the bagels before they get cold?"

But he was smiling as he said it.

Harlequin Romance ®

brings you

HOLDING HERO ★ OUT FOR A

Some men are worth waiting for!

Every month for a whole year Harlequin Romance will be bringing you some of the world's most eligible bachelors in our special **Holding Out for a Hero** miniseries. They're handsome, they're charming but, best of all, they're single! Twelve lucky women are about to discover that finding Mr. Right is not a problem—it's holding on to him!

Watch for:

#3415 THE BACHELOR'S WEDDING
by Betty Neels

Available wherever Harlequin books are sold.